Purgatory: Making the Champion

Mick MacNeil

Published by Nosepeople Productions, 2022.

PURGATORY: MAKING THE CHAMPION

First edition. March 17, 2022.

Copyright © 2022 Mick MacNeil.

ISBN: 978-1777158163

Written by Mick MacNeil.

Table of Contents

To those who read and enjoy this story.

Let me know: penman@nosepeople.ca

Chapter 1. Dreamer

Sometimes Dante would dream, and in those dreams, he remembered, it was always the same. It was him, of that he was certain, him, but in almost every way, a stranger. That Dante, wearing medieval battle garb, sat astride a strange, horse-like creature. A large sword hung from his hip. In the dream, this Dante was confident in his skill with the weapon. Beside him, astride another oddly familiar, but strangely odd horse like creature, was a large, muscled, silver-haired man. Like a god, Dante thought. Ahead in his dreams, Dante sensed a fierce and relentless enemy just out of sight. Behind him followed a multitude of mounted, battle-ready warriors.

The sleeping Dante sensed a vast legion of approaching enemy was just ahead, but he couldn't see them. The Dante in the dream could. He raised his arm and the ranks behind him reigned to a stop. The god-like giant; the one Dante thought of as the golden man turned to face him and smiled. The golden man pulled his sword from its scabbard at his waist and held it before his face in salute, blade pointing skyward, then turned his mount, riding back to join the array of warriors waiting behind.

There was something approaching through the mist ahead. Dante lowered his arm, and a roar came from those who followed. Dante whispered into the ear of his steed, and it galloped forward. As one, the massed army behind him surged with him. The feeling was indescribable. Just as his hand dropped to draw his sword, Dante would wake up.

Dante didn't understand the dream, but he loved it. The confidence, the sense of power the dream provided him, would sometimes linger for a few delicious moments. After that, the real world reclaimed its place. He wasn't Dante, swordsman, cool and bold, the commander of an enormous army. Instead, he was Dante; the kid exempted from physical education by his parents. He was the boy who could play no sports. When his friends had water gun fights, he was the wet one holding his parents' one concession, a rubber duck that sprayed water through a hole in its bill. It was the only thing remotely gun-like his parents would permit.

In high school, Dante's parents tried to continue his Phys. Ed. exemptions but were told the subject was integral to the program and so he participated. Uncertain and inexperienced, Dante felt awkward and uncomfortable in the program activities. While he saw himself as clumsy, many a coach, looking on would say to themselves or to anyone around, "That boy, looks awkward out there, but he has something. I could teach him to be a competent member of my team," whatever sport it might be.

They would send Dante home with papers seeking parental permission for him to sign up for the varsity basketball squad, or baseball team, or track team, or volleyball or rugby. Every time his parents would tell him no, because this sport, or that sport, was too dangerous.

As he grew older, it became more difficult for his parents to prevent him from joining some of his friends beyond reach of the home, but by that time, Dante had little confidence in his ability to perform any remotely strenuous physical activity. He avoided even the tamest of sports and an extended walk in the park tired him. By the time he graduated from college, he was considered by anyone who knew him as a nice guy with a good sense of humor, fun to share a drink with, but they all thought him a little soft especially when it came to anything remotely athletic.

Academically, he did well and when it came to his studies and the skills for success; he was well above average. He was able to move between a wide variety of courses of study with ease. Unfortunately, only a scattering of this filtered into his self-perception. Still, the friends he had made were intensely loyal and happy to spend time with him. He was a calming influence on the impulsivity of his two closest companions, Adam, and Earl.

The dreams of the other Dante, brave fighter, commander of warriors, fellowship with a god persisted as Dante grew older. He would love to be that Dante, but he recognized it was not who he was, nor was it likely that he would ever even come close. To him, that Dante was extraordinary; the real Dante was just ordinary. Aware he would never meet the Dante of his dream, let alone be him, he made a conscious decision to block the very idea from his thoughts. On waking he would turn his mind to what he could do. He would focus on school then look to find a satisfactory job and when he had it, do it well.

His effort to forget the dream was effective. By the time he was donning his hood and gown and standing before the university chancellor to receive his sheepskin, Magna cum Laude, no less, no trace of the dream remained in his memory or in his consciousness. He was focused on his daily life, which he saw as remarkable only in its being completely unremarkable.

His pragmatic side had no use for such a dream. His adventurous side had diminished to the point where even such a fanciful dream had no place. Dante was no longer a dreamer.

If dreams are windows into the soul, what was it Dante had pulled the curtain down on?

Chapter 2. Vast

Standing on the parapet of his winter castle, Grand Duke Davlos, a wide smile only somewhat obscured by his flattened fangs, surveyed his surroundings. "This is," he exclaimed, spreading his arms, as if to engulf the scene before him, "A vast and glorious domain."

His secretary, Rombir, and his consort, the Duchess Clarvita, nodded and mirrored his grin, but their eyes were more for each other. A few steps behind, Davlos' favorite concubine Astrada, her eyes cast submissively towards her feet, watched from the corner of her eye, a look of amusement playing across her delicate features. The domain was vast and glorious. Despite the ever-constant light mist that never appeared to fade or to thicken, they could observe the richness of the populous land.

That it was enormous was beyond question, for unlike the countless worlds it served, the horizon stretched as far as could be seen. There was no curvature to obscure the distance, only the individual visual sharpness of the one looking. This place with its many sentient species and cultures was special. It was purgatory; the place set between the world of the living and heaven or hell.

This was where the dead waited to be escorted to their ultimate destination. In purgatory two gigantic discs, one of intense brightness providing the illusion of constant daylight and another far darker, constantly pulsing with the shadowed

5

colors of flame, dominated the sky. These were not discs, but circular portals, portals that could be seen, unchanged and unchanging, across the eternal distances.

Here, the dead waited for what might be moments or what might be eons for the terrifying creatures from one or the other portals to gather them to their ultimate destination. Devil or angel, demon or spirit of light, those about to be taken trembled and screamed in terror. The others who could only see their horrific responses did their utmost to escape the scene, cringing as they moved away, their eyes wide and their faces pale. The trembling, pleading, and frightened screams of horror made it clear in their final anguished throes those who transported them, whether angel or demon, were hideous in their aspect.

Souls of those seeking atonement having died in their own worlds awaited their allotted time, lived healthy in reanimated versions of their former bodies. In purgatory, their existence was as real to them as the one they left behind. These made up most of purgatory's population, countless beyond imagining.

What might be more surprising were the many living who also inhabited purgatory. These, or their ancestors, had come through the various passages existing between there and their multitudinous worlds. This occurred over the eons as worlds came and went within their particular universes. Throughout time, souls, alive and dead, from countless worlds, universes, and dimensions found their way to purgatory. Most came after living out their days in their own world, but many of the living had found their way in through a passage and many more were born and lived their entire lives there.

The Grand Duke Davlos was a living being. His ancestors had entered through a passageway along with countless others and had formed a large and powerful Duchy over which Davlos now ruled.

In protecting the borders of his domain, Davlos also preserved the distant reaches of purgatory from being overrun by those who would seek to expand their dominions. He held in check the power seekers who would cross the deserts and deep forests and enormous and impassable swamps where there were many domains ripe for conquest.

Davlos was more than satisfied to rule his domain and fight his internal wars with minimal expansion. Many nearby were already conquered by Davlos' people or by equally warlike and allied species from more ancient and vanished worlds. Over countless generations, under Davlos and his progenitors, a firm but fragile truce had been established and maintained.

The populous of Davlos' dominions, both living and dead while fierce and warlike by nature, in their vast numbers respected their ruler's truce. The beings from heaven and hell rarely came among them. Lives, especially with Davlos' species, were long, death even longer. When the living in purgatory died through misadventure, they returned physically unchanged to a familiar location where they would begin seeking atonement.

Those experiencing their first life could on very rare occasions fall victim to illness. More often they died violently. The atoners were free from all disease. Deaths sometimes occurred among the atoners, but always through violence. They would reanimate in a familiar location and their atonement continue.

Astrada may have been Davlos favorite concubine, but he had many. These concubines were reputed for their timeless beauty, their loving nature, and their sexual prowess. Stolen as adolescent girls from numerous worlds, many looking very much like earthly humans. This was a look, it seems, that was quite popular among a wide variety of human and non-human species they would be seized and carried off to the slave masters' world where they were trained as courtesans and sexual slaves. Scientists there did what they needed to guarantee these girls a delicate beauty and to prepare them surgically to provide sexual pleasure for those from a score of different worlds and species. Once complete, they would categorize and sell them to the highest bidders, or to a favorite customer such as Grand Duke Davlos. They had abducted Astrada and her twin Telastra from their home world as adolescents.

The slavers often frequented purgatory with their wares. It was the choicest location to find the widest array of customers. That is where they brought Astrada, her twin Telastra, and other girls because that is where they would get the best price. Astrada and her sister exhibited a rare delicate beauty and received many bids as they stood naked on the chill stone of the slave market stand. Grand Duke Davlos was one of the biggest buyers that day. Besides the twins, he purchased twelve other girls. Some for himself and some to reward his friends or as benefits to keep those closest and most loyal to him, close and loyal.

Although none could immediately detect it in her manner, Astrada differed from the other of Davlos' newly acquired concubines, even her twin. Davlos' beneficiaries who received his bond and a free hand among the concubines preferred Astrada's sister to the others. They would have sought out Astrada, but she was careful and did her best to stay out of sight when they were around. Under their gaze she would grimace, making a cold and unpleasant expression to dissuade them. Sometimes it worked.

Chapter 3. Revenge

Astrada quietly fumed at Davlos and his courtiers as she saw her sweet and gentle twin, so willing to cooperate with those beasts, subjected to their ongoing cruelty. Astrada's anger grew as she watched harsh and cruel courtiers of Davlos' large and aggressive species began to break her beautiful, compliant sister. They showed no mercy in their quest for satisfaction often causing severe injuries. Eventually her injuries had no time to heal before she would be reinjured again leaving her body broken and her mind soon followed. Her once radiant beauty faded. She looked unkempt and haggard, wandering the corridors of the harem floor of the castle casting frequent nervous glances over her shoulder and muttering to herself. Astrada's twin would pass by without acknowledging her gentle greeting or expression of concern.

Telastra shouted and berated the other girls pulling down favorite pieces of wardrobe from hangers and kicking at them, yelling that no one cared about what they wore just what they could do to them. She screamed at those who confronted her and when the harem supervisors appealed to her to go easy on the others, she would ignore them limping away, speaking angrily to no one in particular and paying no attention to their frustrated scolding. By the time she had reached this stage they decided to lock her up. Left alone in her room, she went silent, lost inside her head.

Seeing this, Astrada, who already hated her enslavement and the surgeries that had deformed her body, came to hate Davlos and his beneficiaries even more for their treatment of Telastra. She held her anger inside and tried to appear to be one of many among the concubines, but she couldn't hide her difference. The average courtesan girl was more interested in her body and her grooming, flashing smiles and trying on gowns and discussing hairstyles, then squealing in delight as called upon. Not Astrada. Very early on she had made her way to the battle arena and watched, a look first of wonder, then of interest at the rough and tumble battle skills of Davlos and his warriors as they practiced. She tried visualizing what she had seen. Her thoughts always ended up with her driving her sword deep into Davlos' vital organs. It was a plan she couldn't resist as she began first to ask, then plead with her master, the Grand Duke to let her share in his military and personal combat practice and learn some of the skills of a warrior.

Davlos first hesitated. She was a concubine built for pleasure, not to train for combat. Aware of his hesitation, every chance she could, she would run up to him, doing a child-like dance of excitement and give him a well-honed innocent schoolgirl look as she begged him to teach her how to fight like his warriors. Her behavior flattered him, and her persistence was so impressive. He finally agreed.

Astrada learned the many forms of personal combat that Davlos, his soldiers, guards, and aides would use when assaulted or during battle. Early on she was clumsy, seeming to trip over her own feet. The soldiers would subdue her with little effort, slapping her on her behind with the flat of their sword when she called, "yield."

As time passed, her techniques improved, but while competent, she did not strike Davlos to be in anyway capable of matching even his weakest rookie guard. She would practice with the apprentice warriors and training slaves. The combat training, they endured was intense and unrelenting, many left the field covered in blood from great gashes inflicted by sword or bruised from brain jarring hits, delivered by clubs and maces, feet and hands. Even after spending a great deal of time working on her skills, Astrada rarely came out a victor in any of her practice battles, and if she did, it was only when a stroke of luck assisted her. On those rare occasions when an opponent moved the wrong way twisting an ankle or a knee, stepped on Astrada's fallen sword or dagger losing balance and falling was she able to earn the cry of "yield" from her opponent.

None of those she trained with ever seemed to notice that no matter how fierce her opposition was, Astrada never seemed to get hurt. If anyone did notice, they would likely put it off to her opponents being gentle with her. They would have been wrong. Unknown to them all, she was observing and absorbing, every move, every technique. While appearing clumsy and unfocused, she was far more skilled and abler than she let on and she knew it. She held back even when she found it hard to do when an arrogant trainee, would slap her with the side of his blade, laugh, and ridicule her with sexual taunts. It was a struggle to resist those idiots, any one of whom she knew she could with a stroke disembowel and then what would that do for their sexual taunts and aggressive inuendo. It was tempting, but she had a plan. She would only reveal her true skill when the right moment came.

After significant time passed, Astrada was ready to reveal to her master what she could do with sword and dagger. She begged her master, the Grand Duke, the best of the warriors in every way, master swordsman, brilliant infighter, excellent archer, on foot or mounted, if he would permit her the opportunity to experience fighting him, the greatest of warriors. Davlos agreed with a lighthearted chuckle confident he would force her within seconds to yield. He would give her a small bit of time to play around then bring the show to the end. If he injured or killed her, oh well. She might be one of his better concubines, but she was only chattel, he owned plenty more.

Before the challenge match with Davlos, Astrada made her way to the room where her sister, Telastra, was being held. Her hate for Davlos was almost overwhelming. Why wouldn't Davlos, knowing the way of purgatory, have given Telastra a merciful death so she might at least return to the part of purgatory that was the domain of her home world. Astrada could only watch from beyond the door, unable to get close to the failing Telastra as she held no key to the door. Pressing her face against the bars of the window, she whispered to the unheeding Telastra, tears coursing down her cheek, that she loved her very much and while she could not set her free, she would, this very day, avenge her. The resolution in her voice was shocking, even to her and Telastra turned a surprised gaze towards her sister. Their eyes met and Astrada sensed a brief look of recognition.

Prior to a training session the combatants would choose their weapons from the arsenal beside the training field. Unlike many of the others, Astrada would listen with interest to the weapons master explain what to look for when choosing a weapon. As Astrada's skills and knowledge grew she would secretly make her way to the deserted armory, select from a variety of swords, daggers, battle axes and others. She would face the practice mirror and test her cuts and strokes. Her objective was to find what would be best for her size. She found a sword that felt just right, light, well balanced and with good heft and a dagger with a slimmer and lengthier blade than most. She practiced her moves with them in secret whenever she could until they became an extension of her. In the training sessions she never used these weapons and instead secreted them in a dusty box in a far corner of the room.

Davlos chose a time when the training program for that period was over. For him, there would be no spectators to hoot and jeer as he played with his pet concubine. It was no surprise when Davlos chose sword and dagger for the demonstration challenge. These were his favorite weapons for fighting on foot. What he would never know was these were also the weapons favored by Astrada.

Sent to the arsenal to get her weapons, she strode past the many racked swords along the wall and the shiny daggers matched with them. She went to the distant corner where she had secreted her favorite weapons and opened the box she had placed them in. She withdrew the sword and dagger taking a moment to try some slashes and jabs to testing her comfort with them. After a few feints and moves with the chosen weapons, she took the whetstone to the sword's already keen edge, working it till it was razor sharp. As she sheathed the dagger, its narrow blade gleamed in the subdued light, Astrada couldn't have been more satisfied as she strode, weapons in hand to face her master. It would be, as she well knew, a battle to the death. Either Davlos would die, or she would. Davlos was, of course, unaware of any of this as they crossed blades and he shouted, his version of '

en garde.'

They began to bob and twist, dodging and thrusting with dagger and sword trying to find their rhythm, while two Marshall's looked on, ostensibly keeping score. Davlos began easily, barely moving, thrusting with sword and dagger. He was surprised, her defenses were better than expected as she easily countered each of his moves, dancing away then quickly jumping in with a thrust. This irritated him and he grew more serious in the thrust and slice of his own sword and dagger. Whatever he tried, he found she was meeting his advances skillfully. Unable to land an unblocked blow, Davlos grew more frustrated. Astrada's exceptional defense foiled him at every move. Moving with deceptive grace, she had avoided all his stokes until she seemed to stumble and, in the moment, lose concentration, allowing him to reach in with his blade to strike at her exposed midriff. Astrada made a pained gasp. A brief look of satisfaction crossed his face. He was sure he had drawn blood and expected her to yield. This was just as Astrada had planned. The ruse had worked, she couldn't resist a grin as she began to reveal all she had learned of sword and dagger combat. Instead of crying yield, she attacked more savagely.

In moments, Davlos was on the defensive. So quick and fierce were Astrada's strokes and slashes that he was forced to focus on defense and was unable to offer any serious counterattack. Having grown angry at the ferocity of the small concubine's onslaught and the effort it took to defend against it, he attempted to return her ferocity with a ferocious attack of his own. He drove the sword at her exposed breastplate while slashing low with the dagger to score her leg, sever a ligament and drop her. She feinted away from his sword while fending off the dagger slash with her own sword. Imagine his surprise as she neatly avoided his thrusting sword, deflected the slashing dagger, and leaped toward him driving her sword deep into his chest and through his heart. He collapsed to the ground, his eyes briefly wide and staring in disbelief, then closed as the two Marshalls rushed to his aid.

Neither Marshall would reach the fallen duke as Astrada, in one smooth extended move, drove her sword deep into the heart of one while reaching with her dagger to slash the throat of the other. Both collapsed in death at the feet of their fallen sovereign.

Sheathing both sword and dagger, Astrada ran from the practice room and into the castle. Passing some courtiers on the way, she called to them. "His highness is going to bathe in the practice room and will need some fresh towels after he has spent some relaxing time soothing his aches and pains. He told me to tell you."

As she vanished into a nearby corridor, she shouted at them, "He wants nice fresh towels, soft ones."

With the courtiers heading off to find towels, Astrada raced through the halls to the royal chambers. Throwing open the door, she could, as she expected, see the Duchess sharing a tryst with secretary Rombir. The duchess was at her play, while the duke was at his 'play'. Both Rombir and the Duchess were among Davlos' courtiers who had coldly and cruelly misused Telastra. One thrust of the sword through both writhing bodies was all it took to complete their little escapade and settle the debt they owed Telastra.

With five dead already, the Duke, his Duchess, his secretary and two warrior Marshalls, she would have to move fast before they detected the fallen and before suspicion fell on her. Her position as a weak and fearful concubine and her poor attempts at combat in the practice room might buy her time, but she couldn't be sure.

She raced to the stables where she found her favorite steed, well rested as she had planned, bearing her full pack, and ready for a fast ride across the fields to the swamps. Mounting, she whispered into the beast's ear, and they were off.

She would be well into those swamps before there was any pursuit or at least that was her hope. The swamps, thick forest and badlands between domains was a dangerous and unlikely destination even for the killer of the Grand Duke and, as she wanted to believe, the last place they would look for her.

Chapter 4. Tauren

Reaching the badlands between domains was only the beginning for Astrada. She had a destination and her route carried her across many a swampy and rugged barrier and through numerous domains without ever stopping except to eat or rest as she made her way. After a great deal of time, perhaps a century in earth time, or perhaps only a scant few moments, time in purgatory being relative, Astrada reached her goal at last, earth's domain. There she sought out the local guardian. Every domain had one. Although warriors without peer, a sense of greed had overwhelmed many, making them more interested in gathering wealth and living the good life.

Guardians were native to purgatory and supposedly immortal. They were last to be carried through one or other of the Portals dominating the sky. Most remained faithful to their duty but the rich and powerful had bought off many. Other guardians after a near eternity of watching over peaceful domains were unexpectedly taken by powerful warlords from distant domains. They were placed in forms of captivity designed by master scientists from ancient worlds and kept in an imprisonment unimaginable on earth.

Astrada, in her travels across the many domains, had heard of Tauren, the earthly guardian. The word was he was strong and true and possibly one of the most traditional and effective. Being similar in body type to Astrada, although with the normal differences between male and female, she felt he was one with whom she could train and from whom she could learn. One she could go with side-by-side in battle.

She came to the central city of earthly purgatory to find Tauren, who was said to be training acolytes there. She was directed to the Stade Arcanium. The Stade was a rectangular open-air stadium. Stone steps, the seats for spectators, surrounded an expanse of grass and sand. It was perfect for viewing sporting events, but when Astrada arrived there were no spectators and on the field, a few, mostly younger men, were busy engaged in what appeared to be slapping at each other with dull wooden swords.

In their midst, his broadsword resting on his shoulder, stood the most beautiful human being she had ever seen, His snowy hair flicked against the blade of the sword, his face looked as if etched by a classical sculptor. His golden eyes glinting in the reflected light from a series of mirrors scattered around the field's edge. A well-formed nose neither too big nor too small centered his face. A light smile played across his lips as he surveyed the surrounding swordplay. He was a giant of a man, and his leather kilt and crossed bandoliers couldn't hide the well sculpted musculature of his body. From the top of his silver locks to the soles of his high laced sandals, Astrada could see that he was someone special, a fierce warrior far different from the others. He had to be the guardian.

She made her way through the battling pairs, neatly sidestepping a wild swing here and a fierce thrust there. When she reached the handsome giant, she put her hand to the dagger at her waist and forthright asked, "Are you Tauren?"

"Ah," he exclaimed, looking down at her, "you're here at last! We've been expecting you for some time now."

"Well." Returned Astrada taken aback by this unexpected greeting, but not to be outdone, "I'm sorry I'm late. I didn't realize I was expected."

"Indeed," smiled the giant.

"And how is it you expected me and how do you know I'm the one expected?"

"Oh, I have my ways."

"Which are?"

"If you must know, the Wise Ones contacted me. They told me you would come, a powerful female battle companion, to fight by my side when we wage war on the coming invaders. Something, by the way, they say you precipitated."

"This so-called invasion I apparently precipitated, when will it occur?"

"Oh, not to worry, it is still a long way off. Plenty of time for you to help me train an army and find our champion."

Astrada would learn the Wise Ones, to anyone's knowledge, had no other names, were native to purgatory and had knowledge of the present and future. They spoke only to the guardians when they deemed it needful. They remained hidden from sight in those remote forests and swamps separating the domains.

Astrada knew if any of Davlos' followers suspected her of his murder or the murder of his duchess, their pursuit would be relentless. She didn't fear this. Nor was she that surprised by Taren's revelation she had precipitated a potential invasion. She had a powerful feeling whoever might replace Grand Duke Davlos would be one of the more ambitious of his lords, someone eager to increase his power through conquest.

Chapter 5. Threat

L ord Fluglaz was a cousin of The Grand Duke Davlos. A powerful leader in his own right. He controlled a smaller dominion on the edge of that of Davlos. Davlos empire engulfed Lord Fluglaz and his domain but did not hold it subservient. Lord Fluglaz was a loyal companion of the Grand Duke, one who was more than ready to ride to war with him.

Fluglaz, was always loyal and obedient to the Grand Duke but would often encourage him to move out of his chosen domain and spread his power across all of purgatory. This was beyond impossible because purgatory stretched out to infinity, something neither Davlos nor Fluglaz understood. Conquering its vast reaches was impossible, overwhelming, and unachievable. While the conquest of the unbounded world of purgatory was beyond conceptualizing, let alone achieving, conquest of a large number of domains was not.

Davlos, for his part, was satisfied with his dominion and riding at the head of his armies to quell those few small-scale rebellions that might upset his reign. The idea of any extensive journey of conquest with its forced marches and loss of life held no interest for him.

When Fluglaz brought up the topic, which he frequently did, Davlos would rise from his elaborate throne-like chair, to stride with clear purpose around the room, a relaxed smile on his soft gray lips revealing the tips of his carefully filed fangs. He stepped up to each of his concubines and courtiers alike, fondling their faces, squeezing their shoulders, then would turn to Fluglaz and ask, "Why would I waste my time on the battlefield subjecting staunch and loyal warriors and their brave steeds to injury and death, when I have everything, I could ever want already?"

Lord Fluglaz did not understand Davlos' simple satisfaction, although to be honest, it was far from simple. Davlos ruled over a dominion containing many domains. Unlike Davlos, Fluglaz took little satisfaction in the plenty he already had. He was more interested in growing his power. It was an insatiable hunger for power leaving little thought for the lives of his warriors and their steeds.

While Grand Duke Davlos lived, he held Lord Fluglaz in check. Once Astrada's blade had stopped Davlos beating heart, it gave Fluglaz unofficial license to pursue his quest for greater power. His first act was to seek out any who might prevent him from assuming the title of Grand Duke. There was quite a bloodbath at the palace. Lord Fluglaz had the support of a large number of Davlos warriors as he and his cohort had often joined with Davlos and his forces to put down uprisings that from time to time arose in the more distant regions of the dominion.

Davlos' dominion was a large one incorporating the domains of many worlds. Beyond the borders of the Grand Duchy there were several smaller states which Davlos let keep their independence. Except for the domain of Fluglaz, an associated nation, they had little to do with the Grand Duchy. While grateful for the military support Davlos could provide if they needed it, they were more grateful Davlos otherwise left them alone.

Fluglaz, having claimed the title of Grand Duke could now pursue his dream of conquest and the boundless power that would accompany it. The grateful tributes from the smaller states thanking the Grand Duke for his support and his leaving them their independence was not enough for Fluglaz. After consolidating his power within the boundaries of the Grand Duchy, he set out to expand the dominion. His first successful conquest came at the expense of the surrounding smaller states.

These states, so protective of the independence they had gathered around themselves like a warm and fuzzy blanket during Davlos' reign, were unable to present a united front in time to stand up to the greed of Fluglaz and the strength of his forces. Fluglaz's forces easily overran each, one after another. Their tiny forces no match for the massive military might he could call upon.

Before long, Fluglaz dominion covered all the realms of similar sentient species from the same universe of origin. While now controlling a dominion beyond human concept, it was not enough. His desire for absolute power drove him to cross the swampy boundaries into the far-reaching domains of different universes. their countless worlds, and their many sentient species.

To one side of Fluglaz's domain were a several near empty domains belonging to abandoned worlds and dimensions where the civilizations and sentient life forms had long since ceased to exist. Most of the few who remained in these ancient domains of purgatory were atoners, there to complete their atonement. With little effort any one of Fluglaz's growing number of legions could claim and hold several of these which is exactly what happened.

To the other side of his dominion were domains of younger worlds. Among these were several domains Fluglaz was able to overpower and win through bribery and control of the local guardians. Those that resisted fell to force of arms. One of Fluglaz legions, while still many domains away, was making its way toward the domains of Earth and its associated worlds.

Thanks to the flexibility of time in purgatory, Tauren and Astrada would have the time to seek out and train a champion and prepare skilled warriors who could skillfully defend the domain from a conquering army. Besides the many among the living who had or would make their way through one or another of the passageways prepared to serve, there were centuries worth of warriors, soldiers, and the battle hardened ready to stand in defense of their domain while they awaited the finish of their time of atonement. Many of those who answered Tauren's call did so in the hope that standing in defense of their domain along with the guardian and the champion, whoever he might be, would improve their chances for the light.

As yet, there was no champion around whom to rally, although some, impressed by the warrior skills of Astrada, felt she might be the one. While she looked like the humans of earth, she was not. The champion had to be human, and he or she had yet to be found. This was the task assigned Astrada and required of Tauren.

Chapter 6. Seeking the Champion

Together, Tauren and Astrada set off to begin the search. Present population estimates for earth was somewhere between seven and a half billion and seven and three quarter billion people. Every single one of these beyond the age of twelve might be the champion they were seeking. Their search was likely to be extensive and take a good deal of time, time being something more crucial to the living earth than to purgatory, but in this case, important there, too.

A champion, on being found, would have to accept her or his role and then go through extensive training. Their search would need to be comprehensive. There was no room for a mistake. The two searchers, working together, would do their best to take a systematic approach. They would do their best to prioritize their search, beginning with the world's top athletes, work their way through them, then proceed down the line of lesser athletes before moving on to the warriors. In most cases they were the soldiers, and the two searchers would begin with the most proficient of these.

After that, if they had failed to find the champion, they would broaden their search to include anyone and everyone. If they didn't find the champion on the first go through, Tauren and Astrada would start over, continuing until they found the required champion. They hoped soon to come across their target among the athletes. The champion should be a natural.

However, it didn't seem to be the case. Instead, it became what they had hoped it wouldn't, a long and tedious search. Even after an extensive exploration, they had not found the one they sought. It forced them to try again. By the third search, Astrada was ready to leave it behind, head back to purgatory and prepare her own army of defense. Tauren, partly out of persistence and partly out of stubbornness, was not ready to give up. "The champion is there, somewhere, and it is for us to find him,"

Astrada grumbled, but remained with him, carrying on the annoyingly complex and involved quest.

Chapter 7. Meeting Dante

"Mom, please, coach really wants me. He saw me run during Phys. Ed. Class and says I'm fast."

"No, Dante," the diminutive woman in the patched peasant dress and straight brown hair showing the slightest touch of grey, shook her head hair momentarily covering her eyes, "you know how we feel about sports. Joining track and field is out. Why not spend more time with the chess club? They have competitions, too."

"But mom, I don't like chess anymore. Anyway, I can beat everyone at school including Mr. Bonini and he played on the competitive chess team at university."

A thin, bearded man wearing a paisley shirt and frayed bellbottoms stepped into the room.

"Here's your father, Dante. He'll tell you the same thing."

"Dad, Coach Jacks saw me run. He wants me to join the school track team for the district tournament."

"Son, you heard your mother. Sports are far too dangerous. Hey Sally, do you remember that guy from the commune, Don Etherly, if I recall his name correctly. Remember, he had been a runner at university."

"Oh yes, he used to tell us about the time he had that terrible accident at the International Colleges' Meet. Poor fellow needed to use two canes to help him get around, his leg was so twisted.

"Crippled for life because of a silly running contest. We will not see that happen to you, son."

"Sports are just too dangerous, Dante. You tell the coach you're sorry, but you can't join."

Dante's parents failed to mention the terrible accident crippling Don Etherly did not occur while he was running but resulted from being hit by a car after the post-race celebration at a local bar. In a similar way, while not always clear on the details, they seemed to know someone in every popular sport who was seriously injured, in an often near fatal accident due to their participation in the sport.

In the short time Dante took part in gym classes before his parents were able to have him excluded, he showed natural athletic skill. Through elementary school and well into secondary, coaches, on seeing him perform, usually only once, were frothing at the mouth to add him to their particular team. Dante would have loved to take part in any sport. He never did, and by about the third year of secondary school, the coaches had given up and so had Dante.

By the time he finished college and went off to work at a large insurance firm, no coach would even take notice of the slightly pudgy, poorly conditioned man he had become. It had reached the point when asked in passing if he cared to participate in the fun team building sports activities, Slo Pitch, Broom Ball, or other sporty activity his fellow workers enjoyed, he would always decline. Not that he was unsociable. He often attended the events as a spectator and joined his fellows at a local watering hole for a post-game drink.

Dante was not a total failure. He was exceptional at his job, friendly and always good with associates and fellow workers.

As section manager, he was a favorite with everyone in his department. He was a popular and likeable boss, a rarity even among the other managers and superintendents in a company reputed for its amiability and being a great place to work.

He was equally popular with the women on staff who found him shy and reserved and likely a good catch for the right one. His parents had warned him many times of the risk of jumping at the first skirt that showed an interest in him, encouraging his already extreme shyness. "Be careful, Dante, there are women out there who will take advantage of you. They'll take your money and leave you."

The attitude of Dante's parents was odd for a couple who had met at a hippie style commune. They had come together among the smoke of firepits and the fog of recreational drugs. Dante had been born there, but his parents had left the commune shortly afterward. What never went beyond the two of them was a dream they both shared in which they each heard a voice, its message prompting them to leave the commune forever. The voice they heard gave them a pointed three-word command, "Protect the child."

That was all it said, but they had taken it to heart and left the commune to find a more protective life. They had named their son Dante, but it wasn't because they were lovers of literature or poetry, in fact, they had never heard of Dante's Inferno. His parents named him after the drummer in a psychedelic band they liked. It seemed like a good name if perhaps a little different.

Despite everything, Dante's dad got an excellent job. It seemed miraculous, but neither Dante's dad nor his mom questioned it. Soon they were well-housed if somewhat oddly dressed suburbanites. Their ultimate mission was to safeguard their son. Since they didn't have any idea what they were to protect him from, they sheltered him from everything. Much to Dante's chagrin, either mom or dad would drive him to school and then pick him up after to bring him home. There was no afternoon play time outside the house or with those dangerous young people who, with great reluctance, they let him spend the school day.

Although his parent's goal in obedience to the dream message was to protect him, Dante couldn't understand why he was prevented from ever participating in any sport. He was sure if he did too well in chess, they'd be pulling him out of that with stories of how someone at the commune, in a moment of concentration over a chess board, inhaled a pawn and could have choked to death.

Chapter 8. Closing In

D ante sat between two work friends, Adam and Earl, the three gazing at their reflections in frothy glasses of beer. While across the table, Marilee, a goblet of white wine in her hand, was laughing with some other women from the office. All those women, but none of the men could see she kept a protective eye on Dante. While no one was ready to consider it, there might be a look of ownership in the glance. If confronted, she would deny it, and none would be the wiser. Except, on closer inspection, a perceptive person such as Tauren, if he were looking, could see the signs were there.

As this was happening, the quest for earth's champion dragged on. Tauren, wearing a well-tailored grey suit with a cranberry-colored tie, looked like a giant business executive. Astrada, wearing a dark, rather stiff looking pantsuit, was stunning and despite the conservative nature of her outfit could not hide the fact that she was supremely hot. In fact, she had drawn so many stares, although no one seemed brave enough to include a wolf whistle, she was sorely tempted to remove the next head turning to give her the eye.

After so many days of this, Astrada was ready to leave this annoying world to its own devices. The turned heads, the constant staring, all those who stopped and stood aside to watch the two pass had become too much for her. Although the attention didn't seem to bother Tauren, he recognized

Astrada's discomfort. "I can take care of this if it's getting on your nerves," he said, a smile playing across his lips.

"If you can do this, then stop your bloody grinning and take care of it," snarled Astrada.

Tauren waved his hand. It looked like a meaningless gesture to Astrada, but after that, the excessive attention stopped. "Are we invisible?" she asked.

"Actually, no," Taren returned, "Just not very noticeable. If we were invisible, people would walk into us, but in this case, they know we are here. They see us, they just don't pay any attention to us."

With one problem solved, there remained a more persistent problem as yet unsolved. Where was the champion and would they ever find him or her? At the moment, it was looking more unlikely.

Together Tauren and Astrada had journeyed through every part of the earth, every continent, every country searching for the champion, whoever he or she might be. They had scoured their way through the populace of cities and villages, visiting the places where they would find the strong and capable, physical specimens, athletes, and soldiers. Many they came across might be of great help in the battle for earth's purgatory, but none could claim the title of champion. "How do you know none of them are the champion?" Asked Astrada through clenched teeth, "surely one of them has to be?"

"Sorry," said Tauren, "but I will know. And we have yet to encounter the one. We must be looking in the wrong place."

"Where else would you look for a hero, but among the warriors and the fit and well-conditioned?" asked Astrada, holding out her arms in frustration.

"Don't know, "returned Tauren, "but time is running short. We must keep looking."

Currently, they were walking along a street in a smaller city somewhere in the northeastern portion of the North American continent. It might have been place like a Kingston or Windsor in a part of Canada called Ontario, or Grand Rapids in Michigan, USA or Syracuse in New York, USA. It was all the same to them, although they did think it odd that these places had such long names. Their only reason for being there was to find earth's champion, a hero who would help save earth's purgatory and prevent an invasion of earth itself.

Astrada had to admit the people of earth were, in their own way, a colorful lot, not just in their looks, but in their works. As she walked down the street in this small city, she couldn't help but look around her with interest. The many-colored vehicles, the variety of costume, the light from gaudily decorated windows and the many buildings, all similar in shape, but also different from each other amazed her. She wondered what it would have been like had she been born into this world.

She understood it was far from perfect. The impoverished and homeless she had seen in her travels with Tauren, the glib and harried and the glimpses of evil told her this world was not without its serious problems. The difference for her was the range of human attitudes and behaviors. Her world and the world where they turned her into a courtesan and the domain of purgatory where she resided was a place more given to an attitude of black and white. Her long-time home she saw as a place draped in evil, the good there only circumstantial.

Those who were the true inheritors of purgatory were a gloomy lot, busy seeking atonement and in dread of their final call. They were not impervious to physical suffering or even death before being taken into the darkness or the light. Death resulted in their reawakening back wherever their journey of purgation first began.

The living who had found their way through the many portals arrayed among the worlds and dimensional plains were in purgatory either seeking refuge or to exploit the unwary. Unlike this earth with, to Astrada, its simple joys, there had been for her no such middle ground in her world. The endless variety she encountered here on earth searching for the champion, made it difficult to stay focused. She had to force herself to keep her attention fixed on the present moment and on the task bringing her here.

At this moment, neither in the past, nor the future, but right now, she was walking with Tauren along a street of shops, bars, and restaurants in a small city. It was evening, a time more given to visiting shops, bars, and restaurants, than were the early hours of morning, or the time during the day when many of the local denizens toiled at something, they called jobs, or work, along with some more colorful names.

They may now be on their sixth trip around the world searching for this well-concealed champion, but Astrada continued to marvel at the surrounding sights. Where they walked, an earlier rain left a patina of colors on the concrete and asphalt reflecting the colors of the shop windows. To Astrada, the street was a shimmering multicolored work of art. All the hues of the spectrum, the reds and blues, yellows and greens danced around her. For one who had lived most of her life in purgatory where the only colors seemed dull and contrived, this unmotivated artistic free-for-all delivered by an unconscious nature appeared miraculous.

Despite her delight at the small and enticing vagaries of this strange little world, Astrada was growing more frustrated at their failure to locate the champion they so tirelessly sought. When Tauren veered from their path along the sidewalk, making his way towards the door to a tavern, she was, now, both peeved and confused. "I thought you didn't need to eat or drink. Are you looking for something to boost the spirits?"

Tauren didn't respond, pushed open the tavern door and held it so Astrada could catch up. He strolled purposefully towards the rear of the place and took a seat close to a mixed crowd who knew each other. They were sharing laughter and conversation. Enjoying a wide variety of drinks in various sized glasses and munched on finger food from several strategically placed baskets.

Astrada sat down at the table beside Tauren as the waitress approached. "I'll have an ale," said Tauren "and perhaps one of those red drinks for the lady. We'll eat whatever it is they are eating," he added, pointing to the basket being shared by those sitting closest to them.

"One beer, one red wine and two pounds of suicide wings," said the waitress. She was a tall, willowy blond wearing tight shorts and a yellow t-shirt on which was printed the name of the tavern in florid green Celtic print.

The indifference she had brought with her to the table melted as she studied the silver-haired giant more closely. The smile that crossed her attractive youthful features could have lit up the room, but vanished at the sight of the drop dead, gorgeous brunette seated with him. "Yes sir," she stuttered, "they're on their way."

"Why are we here?" asked Astrada.

Tauren appeared to be watching the crowd of revelers beside them and showed with his hand she needed to watch with him. He turned briefly to smile at the waitress, and she giggled as she set down the tankard of ale in front of Tauren and the wine in front of Astrada. A second waitress brought the basket of wings a moment later.

Tauren continued to focus on the noisy crowd at the tables beside them. Astrada reached into the basket and took out a wing. She didn't mind the greasiness as she was used to eating with her fingers. With her first bite, however, her expression changed from peeved boredom to surprise. "What in the demons' circle is this thing?" She shouted in panic as she jumped to her feet, kicked back her chair, and spit the piece of chicken to the floor. "I swear it is on fire. Is my mouth aflame?"

She grabbed the glass of wine and inhaled a cooling mouthful.

Some of those sitting nearby stopped their talk to glance at the momentary disruption. Others, more engrossed in their conversations, didn't notice.

"Sit, Sit," said Tauren, indicating her chair, "It is merely the spices they have added to the pieces of poultry to increase the flavor."

"You call that flavor," hissed Astrada as she signaled for another glass of wine.

"You may have my tankard of ale if you wish. It should cool your mouth more than the wine, I think."

Not waiting for the waitress to bring her the second glass of wine, she did just that. Ale she knew, and it was deliciously cold. It calmed the burning in her mouth and when the waitress arrived with the wine, Astrada held up the tankard. "I'll have one of these instead," she said.

While Tauren sat gazing at the boisterous group beside them, Astrada finished the first tankard and grabbed for the second, chasing the first mouthful from it down with another taste of chicken wings. She decided the spicy bits of meat were fine when accompanied by the amber fluid that filled the tankard. Having just struck this happy balance, it disconcerted Astrada when Tauren jumped to his feet, reached over to grab her arm, and said, "Let's go."

She took one last sip of the amber drink and took the last wing from the basket. She took a bite of her chicken wing, dropped the rest on the table, and followed Tauren towards the door. Just ahead of Tauren, three of the men who had moments before been sitting with the boisterous crowd were making their way through the door and into the street.

Walking out, Tauren pressed two bills into the server's hand and thanked her for looking after them so well. As the two most beautiful people she had ever seen walked out the door, making her wonder if they were famous celebrities and she should know them, she looked at what the good-looking giant had given her, two brand new hundred-dollar bills.

She would discover they were genuine, at least according to the infrared Counterfeit Scout next to the cash register at the end of the bar. The tab may have been sixty dollars or less, meaning she would be flush with tips this evening.

Outside, the three who had preceded them were making their farewells. Tauren walked past them and proceeded to the shop next door and made as if he had seen something very interesting in the window. "You a big fan of baby toys?" asked Astrada, joining him to look in through the window at a large display of infant pull toys and stuffed animals

DESPITE DANTE'S LACK of tone and fitness, his parents succeeded in their style of keeping him protected. He had never been subject to a case of the mumps or the flu and neither chicken pox nor measles or, for that matter, any other traditional childhood illness. He had not even experienced a bad sprain or needed stitches. His physical examinations all concluded that he was very healthy and his immune system sound.

Despite his being timid and his lack of participation in office sports activities, he was well-liked by his coworkers. He was always ready to join the guys and girls at the local watering hole. Many of those girls secretly eyed him and hoped he would show some genuine interest. They all enjoyed being around him. He was interesting and funny and knew enough to carry on a conversation on the many topics that might come up after a few drinks at a social event.

Dante had no plans for a relationship with any of the young women he encountered at work or in his social life. He was, however, developing a friendship with a lovely young lady at work, Merilee Draeger. The administration had recently made Merilee Dante's supervisory assistant. He soon learned Marilee was pleasant and personable as well as efficient and industrious in the workplace, and that appealed to Dante. What's more, she was also both smart and fun at social events.

For the time being, it satisfied her to befriend Dante and keep their relationship distant and platonic. She was well aware of the others who showed interest in Dante, a well-placed and eligible bachelor. While she knew Dante was not ready to even think about getting too close, she was OK with this. At the time, she was not prepared to commit either. As Dante's assistant, however, she was solicitous and ever supportive, insinuating herself into his workaday life, perhaps hoping something might develop down the road. In the meantime, she was a pleasant and fun companion, a diligent co-worker and loyal friend. Dante did, in fact, enjoyed working with her. With no deeper expectations, it was the perfect relationship. Dante discovered he looked forward to those times she came around.

Chapter 9. Kidding

"That's him," said Tauren.

"Who!" Exclaimed Astrada turning to look at the three friends from the tavern, two of whom walk past them along the street while the third set off in the opposite direction.

"That's him," said Tauren again, adding, "quick let's follow," and started off after the lone walker.

Although they remained well back of him, Astrada could see he was one of the men from the loud group at the tables near where they had been sitting. Earlier she had briefly glanced his way, only to see that he was quite unremarkable. He had appeared to her as soft and in poor condition, even compared to the ones with him. The best she could say was that he seemed mildly pleasant looking, and more restrained than some of the others. All in all, he was the last person one would ever suspect of being of heroic or champion caliber.

Tauren, Astrada quickly discovered, intended to follow this person home wherever his home might be. She was not thrilled about it. Tauren was so intense about this, he wouldn't listen to her and her very sound and reasonable arguments why this was foolish. He continued to follow at a distance, far enough to not be obvious, but close enough to see if he should turn a corner, dart into an alley, or enter a building along the way.

Fortunately, the last of the three choices was exactly what he did. He entered a building along the way. Astrada had developed a good common knowledge of spoken English among many other languages. Her reading skills were not as good. Why anyone would enter a building called 3025, Bachelor Apts for rent, she had no idea. Tauren waited briefly at the bottom of the steps leading up to the door the one they were following had gone through.

The building was, to be blunt, nondescript. A faded red brick face featuring a large brown wood framed doorway with a glass door. Above the door, rising up at even intervals, were five wood framed windows. The glass in the upper windows appeared dull and uncared for. The glass in the front door was cleaner and clearer. A planter stood on either side of the door that might have provided a splash of color in the warm weather but was now displaying a couple of dried, colorless stems, the remains of what once would have been charming.

Astrada hoped Tauren's stopping was a sign he had come to his senses and was about to agree with her this poorly conditioned person was not the right one and leave. She soon discovered this was not the case, for, as this thought was crossing her mind, Tauren walked up the front steps and opened the main door. He gestured for Astrada to join him.

They found themselves in some sort of reception area. It contained little more than a set of mailboxes, a speaker phone, and a second glass door leading to a hallway beyond. The door was locked.

Once again, Astrada felt this was sufficient reason to give up the chase and said so. Tauren's response was, "no, we must follow him. I am certain he is the one we seek."

Tauren placed his hand against the lock and gave a little push. The door swung open. "Could have used that trick," said Astrada, thinking back to her sister locked away in her tiny cell.

Crossing the threshold, the vast array of odors confronting them nearly overcame Astrada's senses. The remnants of a wide range of meals overlaid the smell of carpet cleaner and vague traces of oil paint, all blending with the scents of many human beings busily engaged in the activities of living.

She followed up a flight of stairs to the third floor. There, they passed through another glass door held open with a small wedge, on which was a sign in red reading, "Fire door, please keep closed."

Past the door, they continued down a long hallway lined with several windowless doors until Tauren came to a stop in front of a door which to Astrada appeared no different from any of the other tawdry doors in the poorly lit hallway. Except for the 315 in dirty brass numbers on it, it was no different. "In here," said Tauren, pointing to the door with the 315, "He lives in here."

"Are you planning on confronting this human now," asked Astrada who felt some concern about Tauren pushing open a locked door and the terrified response the surprised resident would have at the sight of her and the blond giant casually strolling into his home.

"No," said Tauren, "he's not ready. He has had alcohol, and it dulls the human mind. He could not understand what I am telling him and by morning would believe it was nothing more than a strange dream."

The plan, Tauren explained, was to wait a day or two then draw him through to purgatory and there tell him what was to happen. "What is to happen?" Asked a curious Astrada.

Tauren would open a flexible portal from the bed to purgatory, something he could do because this was the champion and draw him through when he lay down at night. Once in purgatory he would explain to the champion his role and the training he would have to go through, then each night bring him through to work on his conditioning and combat skills.

"Won't he still think he is dreaming," asked Astrada, "can we accomplish anything with him like that."

"Absolutely," smiled Tauren, "in fact, until he is ready it will all be a distant dream. It is most likely he will have a limited memory or even no memory at all of our sessions when he is going about his normal daily routines."

Tauren and Astrada returned to purgatory through one of the local portals, a small green doorway at the end of a narrow alley between two older buildings, one a fly-by-night hotel the other with a remodeled interior made up of middle grade offices. A place where Startup technology companies shared floors with psychologists, dentists, and design consultants among other things.

Shortly, they had returned to the enormous metropolis that filled much of earth's purgatory and was the final homeland to most of humanity, their lives having ended on earth and who now were seeking final absolution. For those who were still among the living and had made their way there from the upper world or from a distant dimension or universe, earth's nether world was a sanctuary. Humanity was far from perfect, and this was a place where sinners made atonement for their wrongdoings. On the whole, however, those seeking atonement, if their stay on purgatory was any length at all, were far gentler, and far calmer than those of a vast number of other worlds.

Different from these other domains, few had come through the earthly portals to exploit it, so it was a peaceful place offering a haven for many species. The center of this great city were the buildings and practice fields home to the guardian of the realm. In this case, Tauren. Here is where he returned, Astrada with him.

While Tauren would go back to earth to find a unique pathway for the newly discovered champion, Astrada would prepare a training program for him. They both agreed that given his conditioning, this would entail a good deal of planning, preparation, and hard work for Astrada as it would also be a long and difficult pathway for the champion.

As Tauren proceeded back to earth Astrada for the first time, but far from the last, saw the task before her and for the flabby, weakling Tauren had declared was the champion they sought, as an impossible one. Nonetheless, she began to take an inventory of what was available and how she could use it to negotiate the plan. A simple one, prepare a poorly conditioned and uninspiring human to face down the fiercest of enemies, far more ferocious than anyone from earth had ever encountered.

Tauren had his own work to do back on earth. He needed to contrive a portal to one of the practice arenas of his home world. While the champion, Dante, was at work, Tauren entered his apartment, a dingy affair with bargain basement furniture, a sofa and a reclining chair that faced a large and expensive flat screen television. Little more adorned the living room. A combined kitchen, dining room held a Formica topped table that in no way matched the Formica topped counter or the chrome silver stove, or the white, double door refrigerator.

The cupboards were neat and orderly, the consequence of a limited amount of crockery and food preparation items. The table was cleared. A mug in the sink close to a quarter full coffee maker was the only sign of life. The champion appeared to like order, a good sign to Tauren. Like the rest of the apartment, the bathroom and bedroom were stark, with the barest of essentials neatly placed on a small dresser in the latter and on a shelf below the mirror in the former.

Tauren thought to place the portal doorway in the doorway to the bathroom, then thought better of it. It would be disconcerting for everyone for the champion to show up in the training grounds desperately needing to void his bowel or his bladder.

After much thought, Tauren decided to use the bed. The champion would lie down on the bed and instantaneously find himself on a pallet in a training arena in the heart of purgatory. Unfortunately, this would mean the champion's sleep time would be dedicated to intense physical activity. Still, there was no way around it. When the champion went to his bed, there was likely no one around to observe him vanishing, or transitioning back. Tauren knew the champion lived alone and from his observations, rarely had anyone in for any length of time.

The portal set, Taren returned to purgatory and Astrada to await the initial visit from earth's newly discovered champion. Time might be of little consequence in purgatory, but for Astrada, the wait for Tauren to return seemed interminable. When he finally arrived, he was alone. "Where is our champion," Astrada wanted to know.

"He should arrive shortly," said an unconcerned Tauren, and he went about setting up a pallet in one corner of the smaller arena.

"Why are you setting up a bed? You have never slept once since we first met." Astrada was confused.

"Just don't want our champion to injure himself transitioning from his home." Moving the pallet ever so lightly, he looked up, "There, that should do it," he said.

Chapter 10. Where Am I?

Dante could barely keep his eyes open as he stepped through the door of his apartment. He had a long day at work. He was socializing with some of the office gang the previous night and had very little sleep. He stifled a yawn as he hung up his jacket in the hall closet. He could feel his bed calling him. He kicked off his shoes and removed his already loosened tie, pulling it over his head and dropping it on a small table just inside the door. He looked into the kitchen, but decided he was just too tired to make anything to eat. Supper could wait until he had a nap. He went to his bedroom and with a sigh lay down on his bed.

What Dante didn't know as he lay down was his bed was now a personal and exclusive portal to purgatory. He had closed his eyes for a moment when he sensed something had changed. The air seemed different, cooler and dryer, and had he forgotten to turn off the lights as it seemed to be a lot brighter than it was when he came into the bedroom. Whatever it was, Dante was satisfied he was in his bed and fell asleep.

"Oh, I can see he's battle ready," smirked Astrada.

A sleeping Dante lay on the pallet Tauren had set for him. A drop of drool glistened at one corner of his open mouth.

For several moments they let him sleep. Tauren and Astrada stood by in silence, while several initiate warriors lounged around the pallet on which their prospective champion slept. Astrada, who on her recent visits to earth had adjusted to the informalities of many languages, grew impatient and in her best American accent said in a loud voice, "O.K. champ, time to rise and shine, you have a lot of work to do, and you need to get started."

Dante's eyes flicked open. Looking around, his head still resting on the gold lame covered pillow Tauren had provided him, Dante felt certain he was dreaming. "Where was he? Who were these costumed people watching him sleep? Who is the tall muscle-bound white-haired guy and the absolutely smashing hottie in the skimpy black costume holding the huge sword?"

It had to be a dream. Dante closed his eyes and rolled over on his side. "Seems you missed the first wake up call, champ," said Astrada, "let me provide some rousing encouragement."

The feminine voice seemed to Dante's ears to blend an astounding combination of sarcasm and command. If that hadn't made him sit up, the painful prick he felt on his neck did. This time, his hand reaching to the pain point on his neck, Dante could take in the total strangeness of his surroundings. And although he still believed he was dreaming, the sight of blood on his fingers added a dimension of reality to the moment.

He turned to gaze at the woman with the sword. He looked at her, then at the sword, then back at her. His tone was incredulous as he spoke. "You stabbed me. I'm bleeding."

"And if it doesn't close up in the next few minutes," she laughed, "you are likely to bleed out from it in a week or so."

Her lack of any sympathy for the distress the wound caused him, prompted him to turn beseeching eyes towards the tall, blond, well-muscled man beside her, 'was he wearing some kind of toga?' He had no idea what he should say, but his mouth of its own volition seemed to have it covered, "Where am I? Who are you people? What's going on here?"

"You're in purgatory," said Tauren.

"I'm dead!" If he had been incredulous before, now he was terrified.

"Well," explained Tauren, "no, you're not dead. You don't have to be dead to come here, although most are."

"Does that mean all of you are dead, then?"

"Well, here, none of us are, although you wouldn't be able to tell even if any of us were."

"And" added Tauren, "who we are? We are your trainers, sparring partners, and, I hope, some of us, your mentors."

"Why me?" Asked Dante, "I haven't even belonged to a gym."

"That's apparent," sneered Astrada.

Dante could think of nothing else to say. It was all so strange. He rose to his feet and surveyed his surroundings. This had to be a dream. The area had a medieval appearance, but not the classic one, more like the medieval look found in futuristic science fiction movies. It was a large open space, like a gym, with a firm but dirt floor. The roof, white stone. held up with columns with their intricate design, making it appear more like it belonged on a monument than a gym.

"What in hell is this place?" demanded Dante.

"Purgatory, not hell," replied Tauren, "a staging ground for hell to be sure, but only for those who have died and are deserving. When they've finished their time of atonement. Tends to be an extended stay for almost everyone."

"No, I mean what's this space we're all in?"

"I suppose you could call it a practice field."

"A sports practice field?" asked Dante.

"If you think war is a sport," snorted Astrada returning her sword to its scabbard.

Dante was dumfounded. "War! Why am I here?"

He couldn't miss the dismissiveness in the hottie's tone. "Why? Because I have been informed that you are the champion of earth and its domains."

"Are all the ladies in purgatory like you?"

"Ladies!" chuckled Astrada, "There is no-one else here or any other place like me."

"Geez, that's a relief!"

"We'll just see how much relief it is. Shall we get started?"

It was obvious the hottie with the sword was not making a request. She withdrew her sword from its scabbard once again, flourished it, then pointed it towards the far end of the enclosed field. "Run to the furthest pillar over there and back to me as fast as you can. Move it!"

Dante gave her an incredulous look. "I'm sorry?"

"Listen, champion," Astrada hissed, swinging the edge of her sword toward his leg, just stopping short of making contact, "get moving before my blade gives you a reason not to run."

A quick glance at her face convinced Dante she was serious and ready to use the blade as she said. Dante ran. Astrada, sword still drawn, ran beside him. Running had never been his thing, even as a child, because his parents forbade it, but he thought he was giving it his best shot. He had not gotten halfway to the pillar before he was breathing hard, and his calves ached. Astrada, however, was doing a relaxed lope beside him. When he slowed, he felt the flat of her sword strike painfully against his thigh. "Keep moving," he heard her shout.

He ran as if his life depended on it. At some level, he was believing it did. It was a long and agonizing run to the far column and back to the group standing beside the pallet he had awakened on, but he made it. He stumbled and fell to the ground beside the muscular giant, wheezing. Astrada was right there with him, looking like she had just taken a relaxed stroll.

Ignoring the prone and wheezing figure, Astrada turned to Tauren. "So, this is your champion. Look at him, he's exhausted after jogging such a short distance."

Tauren smiled, "You have a point, Astrada, it does look like you have quite a job ahead of you."

"I am no miracle worker!"

"You'll do just fine," returned Tauren as he walked out of the square and away from the sullen Astrada and the wheezing champion.

"Yes, fine!" sneered Astrada, turning toward Dante, "Okay champion, while you're down there give me as many push-ups as you can."

It hadn't taken Dante long to realize Astrada was not one to kid around. He adjusted his position on the ground and attempted the very first push up of his adult life. And it was just the beginning, as over the course of the earthly night, Astrada drilled Dante like a demented football coach, forcing him to use every muscle in his body.

As back on earth, morning was approaching, Astrada let Dante take a well-deserved break. He lay down on the pallet as his coach had suggested and moments later, he was back in his own bed, sound asleep and with no memory of his overnight experience.

Not long afterwards, the alarm went off, rousing the champion for another day of work.

Chapter 11. Hurts

The moment the alarm went off, Dante sat bolt upright. He scanned the room to make sure he was where he thought he was. For some reason, unknown to him, he needed to confirm the familiarity of the room. There was no question this was his room, the room he had fallen asleep in. He couldn't understand why this was suddenly so important to him, but somehow it was.

The quick post alarm survey of the room became a regular morning ritual. It was the closest he would come to remembering his time in purgatory. This first morning, however, Dante felt content with himself and his surroundings until he tried to stand up. His knees buckled, his legs were stiff and sore. In fact, his entire body felt stiff and sore. It was, he thought, as if he had run a full marathon while doing some tumbling as he went along.

He staggered his way into the shower and stood under a soothing jet of steaming spray. He noticed the water flowing from him toward the drain had a golden tinge. He had seen it before, but it registered for the first time. It was as if a fine yellow sand had somehow covered his entire body, which it had, although he could not imagine how. Once out of the shower, the stiffness and soreness came back with a vengeance. Dressing was difficult as was the complete process of making and eating breakfast with most of the time spent on wincing and groaning.

Dante was sure he was coming down with something. For someone who had never been sick a day in his life, this was disconcerting if not terrifying. He would have called in sick, but it was month end in his department and without him there the staff members were likely to become anxious about the workload. It was Dante who knew the procedures and often took care of most of it, helping and comforting his harried staff. He knew as surely as night followed day, he would get panicked phone calls from the office every few minutes asking how to do this or that. There would be no rest and doing his job over the telephone did not enthuse him and so he went in.

What was most mornings a pleasant walk to the office was today a slow and painful one as he dragged himself along? This morning, the half mile seemed more like ten. Despite all this, he only arrived a few minutes later than usual. As he entered his department's section, he could see the looks of relief on the staff members. He may be glad he came, but not as glad as they were. The soreness had not abated, making his movements stiff and labored, but it amazed him to realize that while he felt sore, he didn't feel sick.

It was a long and mentally strenuous day, but not physically taxing, and perhaps because of this, Dante didn't feel much better by the time the workday ended. The walk home was painfully slow and once through the door, Dante wanted another hot bath, a quick bite to eat and to crawl into bed.

As he lay back on his bed, he closed his eyes and for a moment flashed back to the peculiar, almost forgotten dream he had the night before. He could still remember the female voice demanding in no uncertain terms he best get on his feet and get working. Then he realized it was not a memory someone was telling him just that. With a reluctance he opened his eyes, afraid he was going to see what he did see. There was the beautiful armor clad woman standing in front of him, her hand on the pommel of her sword which was, thank God, still in its scabbard. Stiff and sore or not, Dante was about to have a serious workout.

For the next couple of days, everything he did was painful, each movement an agonizing struggle. His staff wasn't sure why their fearless leader moved through the office as if he was a cripple, but they could tell he was in pain and sympathized with him. While most treated him with care and respect, Marilee had taken to giving him a neck massage while he sat in his office chair. Under normal circumstance, Dante would have been too timid to accept this, but it felt so good, and she was getting some knots out.

Dante had to say no when the staff invited him to join them at a local watering hole to celebrate the successful conclusion of month's end. A disappointed Marilee offered to drive him home, but he demurred at that. He had accepted her massages but was not yet ready for any other personal attention from her. All he wanted was to have a nice warm bath and climb into bed.

While the bath was running, he went into the kitchen and ate a cold chicken drumstick and drank some milk. Even his jaw was sore. The bath relaxed him enough to take some edge off the soreness. He fell into bed, only to find himself back on the practice field in purgatory.

Astrada was relentless. She was determined to get him into decent physical shape before beginning to train him in any warrior skills. The workouts were intense. He would awake each morning after several hours of workout having no memory of what he had been doing, but his body remembered. The pain was excruciating, bad enough to send him to the doctor.

The doctor examined him thoroughly and found no problem. "Have you been working out a lot lately?" he asked, "because what you are describing is what you would feel after doing a series of heavy exercises."

Dante shook his head. He wasn't the type to do a lot of exercise. The short walk to work and back was about the most of it. As he explained this to the doctor, he had some brief memory flashes of running, doing pushups and pumping weights. These flashes were quick and short lived and disregarded by Dante, who assumed they were nothing more than bizarre thoughts inspired by the doctor's question.

Although he was not aware of doing any exercise, the doctor's explanation helped. Advising that some of the burn was probably from a buildup of lactic acid and the intensity of the pain was something athletes and fitness experts called DOMS, delayed onset muscle soreness, caused by minuscule muscle injuries, offered him some small comfort. A least he wasn't dying. How had this come about? He knew he had done no exercise at all over the past few days. Even if he did exercise, which he didn't, he was sure it would never reach a level of intensity necessary to cause the pain he felt.

After the doctor's verdict that nothing was wrong, Dante felt himself relax. As he left the doctor's office, he let out a long sigh of relief. For the first time in weeks, he had a sense of calm. Whatever was bothering him, it wasn't fatal.

Over the next few weeks, the pain and discomfort remained bad, but then it diminished. The general soreness was almost gone by the morning. He bounced out of bed only to collapse to the ground with intense pain in his right ankle. He could see someone bandaged it but couldn't remember how or where it was done. A further mystery was the brass handled walking stick lying beside him on the bed. He didn't know how or why it was there but when he tried to walk, he was grateful for it. He discovered if he was careful and used the walking stick, he could hobble around the apartment and make his way to work.

The night just past, Astrada had determined the champion was ready to learn some basic hand to hand combat skills. She was Dante's sparring partner and used a variety of simple boxing, karate, and Jiu jitsu moves to knock him every time he tried to get up. At least that's how it felt to him.

The ease with which she could take him down angered Dante, who made a valiant attempt to beat her at her own game and leaped up, fists flailing. He failed once again, but during the simulated fight, he got close enough one time to successfully strike Astrada. It wasn't a very hard hit, as she had mostly blocked it. Her instant response, however, sent him flying across the floor, twisting his ankle as he slammed against a column. The bandage he had awoken to find on his ankle was Astrada's expert handiwork.

The only positive was it returned him to his bed sooner than usual. He got a few extra moments of sleep. Any effect of the extra rest was countered by the agonizing ache of the twisted ankle. This just added to Dante's other ongoing aches and pains that had reduced his already insignificant social life to almost nothing.

Chapter 12. Exhausted

Despite the pain, and there was less than Dante expected, he had difficulty walking. Astrada was not happy with this. The damage was serious enough to make him a useless combat student. She gave Dante a few exercises to build his upper body and hasten repairing his sprained ankle, then sent him back to his home. Finding Tauren, she had to tell him his champion would be out of commission for several days.

The next morning Dante limped into work. His co-workers didn't seem to register this fresh injury. They had grown used to their department head limping around. Although they thought he was getting better, this setback didn't perturb them. The boss's behavior over the past few weeks was odd enough. He was still easy to work with, but he didn't join them in the extra-curricular activities like he used to.

Although he didn't know it, somewhere on a subconscious level Dante was aware this short hiatus from the rigors of his nightly training would be short-lived. He intended to make the most of it. The most of it meaning more sleep. Although he enjoyed his evenings out with the staff, rest seemed a more precious commodity than socialization.

To his own set of staff members, the lack of his presence at their social activities was, at one level, problematic. They liked Dante a lot. As much as he was easy to work for, he was also fun to socialize with despite his timidity. They were wondering if he was becoming more intense and were afraid this might be a harbinger of tougher times for everyone around the office.

His two fellow department heads, guys he had been working and having fun with since even before they joined the company, were also worried. They weren't sure if he was sick or growing old before his time. On the social front as well as in the workplace, he was their leader. While the two of them tended to impulsiveness, Dante was the calming influence in their extracurricular journeys who kept them out of trouble.

Dante just didn't seem interested in hanging out with them anymore. When he wasn't claiming physical fatigue, he was telling them he was just plain exhausted, and he didn't know why. They knew the doctor had given him a clean bill of health but based on the way he looked and what he said, they were unconvinced.

The other thing as one of them expressed was the fact he seemed to have gotten closer to Merilee. She had been hovering over him earlier after he had expressed his physical discomfort. Perhaps he was working out on the sly, hoping to impress her. She seemed impressed enough without the groans of agony that came from their normally inactive friend.

It confused Marilee, too. During the back rubs she provided from time to time, in fact, whenever her duties brought her close, she tried to encourage him to join the group at the next big after work, social activity. A new band and a new comedian were being featured at their favorite watering hole.

Another time it would have interested Dante. He had heard this band was a good one, and the word spread that the new comic's routine was hilarious. But, each time Marilee asked, "I'm exhausted," was the best he could respond.

Give Marilee credit, she was persistent. Everyone was going to the club on Friday. "That gives you two days to rest, and I promise, no one is going to ask you to dance."

Marilee was hard to resist. Dante knew he would enjoy the evening with his friends, and he was finding himself becoming fond of this pretty female fireball. It was difficult to put aside the vague feeling that once his ankle was better, the decent rest he was now getting for the first time in months would end.

After two full nights of sleep the swelling in his ankle went down. Dante's vague misgivings about extreme and ongoing exhaustion faded. This, along with Marilee's regular visits to his desk, convinced him an evening out with his friends, fellow staffers, and her would be just what the doctor ordered, or at least, what the doctor should have ordered. To the delight of all, he agreed to join them at the bar to enjoy the visiting band and share with them a few laughs with the up-and-coming comic.

The evening turned out to be as good as promised. The band was superb, the comedian's set was outrageously funny, and the drinks kept flowing. Well lubricated although not drunk, Dante walked out of the club without stumbling. Not that he could have as Marilee, joining him, grabbed his arm and held on tight. "That ankle must still bother you, I'll walk you home. You don't live too far from me and it's a beautiful evening."

It might not have quite been an old-fashioned walk. The city surrounded them. The roar of busy streets and the bustling Friday night crowds on the sidewalk may have made it less than intimate, but to Dante's mind, it couldn't have been more pleasant. Before long, the two of them were talking and Dante's inhibitions slipped away. He decided he liked this young woman. Not only was she beautiful with her reddish hair and those delightful tiny freckles on her nose, but she was also smart and charming.

It was disappointing to Dante when they arrived at the front of his building. The walk together seemed to be coming to an end too quickly. Swallowing hard, he turned to face her and said, "Well, here we are. Would you like to come in for a moment? I could make some fresh coffee."

To his absolute delight, Marilee gave a slight nod of agreement. Entering the apartment, Dante realized that it had been a few days since he had tidied. Clothes hung on chairs around the living room. He immediately collected everything lying about. "The kitchen is in there. The coffee is right beside the coffeemaker," he pointed, his arms laden down with a week's worth of his unlaundered things, "I'll be right back to make it after I get rid of these."

"I can make the coffee," and Marilee walked past, not seeming to notice his arms were full and stepped into the kitchen.

"No, no, I can make it," said Dante.

"It's Ok, Dante," she said, "I've already found everything."

Dante, carrying the load of clothing, walked into his room. He threw everything into the closet and closed the door and took off his shoes and put on his slippers. He picked up his slippers and sat down on the bed.

"Well," said a woman, her tone bubbling with sarcasm, in a voice, that was not Marilee's, "Our hero has returned."

"No," groaned Dante.

Back in Dante's apartment, Marilee had started the coffee. "This is a nice apartment, Dante. How long have you lived here?"

When there was no answer, she called out, "Dante, are you ok?"

Getting no answer, she walked back through the living room, past the bathroom with its door slightly ajar and empty. She went into his bedroom. "Dante," she called, "where are you?"

Again, there was no response. It was not a large apartment. He should have heard her wherever she was. She revisited the rooms several times until she finally convinced herself Dante was nowhere to be found. "Well, that sucks," she snorted.

She waited around in case he had stepped out to get something or talk to someone and then momentarily return. He didn't. Red faced with anger and confusion, she left the apartment and made her way home. He had walked out on her. Her opinion of the shy department manager changed in that moment. Boy, had she misjudged him. "What kind of a prick would invite her to his apartment, then disappear like that?"

She would have strong words for him on Monday if she spoke to him at all.

Meanwhile, Dante was busily immersed in a sword battle with Astrada. His tactic was to run backwards as fast as he could while trying to fend off the slap of her blade with the sword he somehow was carrying. He hadn't forgotten about Marilee but didn't have time to think too much about her at the moment.

Chapter 13. Catch

Dante's backward scramble across the training room floor didn't protect him from getting a few solid slaps from the side of Astrada's sword. What he didn't seem to notice was how often he was successful in deflecting her blade. Astrada did notice and kept pressing, "Damn it, we don't need a defender, we need him to go on the attack."

If anyone was aware of the earthly expression, "you need to learn to walk before you can run," it was Astrada.

It had taken a good deal of time and patience to develop the skills allowing her to best Davlos, but she was extremely motivated. This was all a complete mystery to Dante, who now and then would pinch himself to test if he was dreaming. Later, having his morning shower, he couldn't help but wonder where he got all those little bruises on his arms and legs.

Astrada's ferocious aggression was the only motivation Dante had at the moment. His concern was more about protecting himself from her taxing practices than about being someone's champion. He had never before participated in any group or individual activity, let alone a competitive one, so Astrada's persistent onslaught was overwhelming. He neither knew, nor cared about being champion of anything? Most of the time, he just wanted to get away from this crazy woman.

Astrada was well aware of this. Tauren had left her with the responsibilities of teaching this least warrior-like of beings not only to fight, but to do so with skill, determination, and ferocity. It was a daunting task. In her mind, she cursed the Wise Ones, whoever and whatever they might be, for giving Tauren advanced notice of her arrival, her warrior skills, and she shivered every time she thought about it, their informing him she had precipitated the coming invasion.

There would be no shirking this duty, but then, Astrada was never one to shirk. She would turn this hapless creature into a superb warrior and do her best to bring out his leadership and motivate him. As she watched him progress with 'baby steps', she knew it would be some time off.

When Dante returned to his bed and his daily life, everything was forgotten. He remembered Marilee coming in. The rest of the evening was a blank. Back at work on Monday, after two days of sleep and two nights of combat training, he came to suspect that things hadn't gone very well with Marilee the previous Friday. He was experiencing something new, a cold shoulder from Marilee that, it seemed to him, could freeze fire.

She didn't look at him. She didn't speak to him. Any work she needed to turn over to him, she let fall without comment on his desk followed by a precise turn away from him and a hasty retreat, head high, back stiff. On the several times over the next few days he tried to approach her. She would turn away, excuse herself and leave, or pointedly ignore him. It appeared as if he would never know what had happened to upset her.

Not only had Marilee frozen him out, but his friends Adam and Earl, likewise unaware of the truth of Friday evening, were driving him crazy with their "nudge... nudge, wink... wink" routine. All Dante wanted to do was shout out to Marilee and his two friends was, "What the hell did I do? and, would you two guys please shut up."

Adam and Earl were department leaders in other sections of the firm. Adam and his group shared the same floor as Dante and his, while Earl's department was a floor below. They were competent in their positions, but away from the job their behavior, to say the least, could be impulsive.

Earl was the more impulsive of the two. During an average workday he would send out countless memos setting goals, listing priorities, and recommending procedures. He would then have to relent and send out as many memos cancelling those particular goals, priorities, and procedures he had earlier announced. Adam, while calmer, was the one who while socializing was more likely to make outrageous comments to strangers.

When out together, they both depended on Dante to keep them in line or to rescue them if they stepped too far over it. This was how it had been since their school days. Dante and Adam had been friends since third grade. Earl had joined the mix in late middle school. They had been fast friends from then on. They attended the same high school and college, and all got business degrees. The two followed Dante around in his job search and ended up working for the same company in the same building.

As Dante went up the employment ladder, his two friends tagged along. When Dante became a senior supervisory officer in his firm, his two friends rose with him taking on similar roles. Dante had no part in their achieving promotions. They performed at their jobs well, were pleasant and personable enough, and the company found their performances more than satisfying.

Colonels to his General, since their childhood they had been the two key satellites to Dante; loyal friends and companions. Once Dante had grown out of his parents' tight control, the three hung together all the time.

They played video games together. Dante liked to play but had no interest in trying to improve his gaming skill, so he wasn't very good. They became familiar with their neighborhood, having often biked together through it in search of adolescent adventure. As they grew older, they wandered through the woods pretending to hunt, smoked there first cigarette behind Earl's dad's garage and later on shared their first joint in Adam's family rec. room when his parents went away for a few days.

Dante did not approve. One puff on the cigarette and he had already decided that this was something he would never do again. He didn't even get as far as a toke on the poorly rolled joint Adam was passing around. The smell overwhelmed him, and he had to leave. Because of Dante's decision, neither Adam nor Earl smoked cigarettes or did recreational drugs. They did, however, like to drink, when they were of age, of course, thanks to Dante's influence. They had developed an assortment of bar bands they liked to follow, and when a celebrity musician or band came to town, they were among the first to get tickets.

As for girlfriends, Adam and Earl had some interest. They dated from time to time. Dante would have loved to date, but he was much too shy. From the time he was a high school junior and throughout university, many girls had shown an interest him. He just couldn't get past his shyness. He could be charming when socializing in a group, and although many of the girls he met there interested him, he never could get up the courage to ask any of them out. "What a snob," was the frequent reaction of those young ladies feeling spurned by Dante.

"Is he gay?" they would ask Adam or Earl.

To Adam and Earl who had often shared their secret skin magazine collection with him, it was a stupid question. They knew that sooner or later he would fall, which is why they thought Marilee was going to be the one. They had seen her head off with Dante the previous Friday but were blockheaded enough to miss her coldness towards Dante on the following Monday.

Meanwhile Dante, who was well aware of Marilee's coldness towards him, had little time to think about it. He was spending his nights in purgatory's Stade Arcanium, working on his combat skills under the critical eye of Astrada. Despite his original awkwardness, she was quietly pleased to see he had refined his defensive maneuvers with the sword and was making some progress with the thrust and slash.

Astrada could tell her student was hitting a plateau in his swordsmanship and decided to try some other skills. Knife throwing was one skill she trained him on. The other was to build his reflexes so he could redirect, or even catch a knife or dagger being thrown at or near him. While he was throwing the knife and after many attempts hitting some part of the target, she had him catching some flat edged practice knives.

Dante's was getting more skillful. He would toss a knife each time getting closer to the bullseye and as he did, Astrada would throw a practice knife back at him. As his movements smoothed out and become more coordinated, Dante was thinking he could handle the real thing. "Throw my knife back to me," he called to Astrada.

For several weeks she resisted, then one day she agreed. Standing beside the knife tossing target twenty meters away, she watched Dante throw his knife and followed its rotation to where it cut into the target just grazing the edge of the bullseye. Quickly pulling the knife from the straw filled target, she made a perfect return toss just to Dante's right. As the knife reached him, his hand flashed out and his fingers wrapped around it. What a thrill, he had actually caught a thrown knife. "Nice catch, champ" shouted Astrada, "but if I may suggest, next time try catching it by the handle."

Dante looked at his hand to see blood gushing around the knife blade in his right hand. He groaned. He had been pain free for so long now.

It was Dante's good fortune that the knife he caught was for throwing, not cutting, or the damage to his hand would have been more severe. As it was, he had a nasty slash across his palm, and it was dripping blood. Astrada, impressed by Dante's newfound if somewhat risky daring, gathered some medicinal unguents and a wrap to bandage his wound.

Chapter 14. Reluctant

One perk of being a champion was quick healing of open wounds. However, it was not something that happened in an instant. On awakening in the morning, Dante discovered his hand, covered in bandaging, was throbbing. Loosening the bandage, he discovered a cut on his palm from just below the index finger to below the little finger. He couldn't remember how he got it, but he knew it had something to do with a knife.

Dante worried that he had been sleepwalking and was handling cutlery while doing so. It seemed clear to him that something happened with a knife. What had he done, dropped a knife and then tried to catch it? Foolish enough, but something Dante felt wasn't beyond him. Whatever the case, he had no intention of letting on that he might have done it while sleep walking. He would take full responsibility. As he told the department secretary, "I was using the sharp knife to cut bread and left it on the counter. When I was shifting my coffee maker to add water, I knocked the knife and it fell off the counter. By sheer reflex, I tried to grab it and caught it by the blade. Should have just let it fall. It wouldn't have hurt anything"

The secretary tsked, but all she said was, "That's an interesting bandage. Did you go to a doctor?"

The bandage was interesting. It was a kind of cloth, but not gauze, something you didn't see often. He told the secretary he didn't think the wound was too bad and didn't bother going to the doctor. Despite that, it was an item of interest for the staff. Even Marilee came by to take a sideways glance at it. When she did, Dante looked up at her and smiled as sweetly as he could.

Marilee turned away. Her back and head seemed more relaxed as she walked away, but still, she walked away. It made him feel a little better. She didn't seem to be as angry with him as she had been earlier.

The fact is that since that evening at Dante's place, she had been wracking her brain trying to figure out where he had gone. The apartment was small. She would have heard the door if he tried to sneak out. She was only a few feet away and he would have had to walk right by her. To the best of her memory, no windows were open. "I should have looked in his wardrobe. Maybe he had gone to Narnia."

The thought caused her to chuckle, but it made as much sense as anything else. She felt less vindictive towards him. She knew he was painfully shy. Perhaps it overwhelmed him having her at his apartment and hid. "Poor guy," she thought, then shook her head, "What am I saying, poor guy? Whatever reason, he did bug out on me."

The same day at lunchtime. Adam and Earl arrived one after the other at his desk, asking if he would like to go out for lunch. Several weeks had passed since what Dante thought of as the Marilee incident. He called it this because during his daytime life he didn't have any inkling what had happened. Dante sensed his two friends wanted to have one more go at him about the Marilee incident, and he was in no mood to face it. His hand was sore, and he was thinking he would rather find a sofa somewhere and grab a bit of shut eye, then fight off the outrageous curiosity of Adam and Earl. He thanked them, saying he had too much to do and would work through lunch.

While his friends knew better, because of their loyalty and respect, they accepted his refusal to join them and left. Dante put his head down on his desk and within moments of their leaving he was fast asleep. As he faded off, he heard a familiar but unidentifiable voice saying, "if I may suggest, next time try catching it by the handle.

The next thing he heard was the concerned voice of Marilee, "Hey, Dante, are you alright?"

Walking by on an errand, she saw Dante was sprawled out across his desk. She tapped him on the arm, but he didn't respond. His arm where she tapped him was firm and muscular. This had surprised her. When she spoke, Dante sat bolt upright, his hair falling over his face, his eyes blinking in confusion. There was something different about him. It was as if she was seeing him for the first time.

Before this she hadn't noticed how chiseled his face was or how his chest and shoulders strained at his shirt. She didn't remember this Dante. Neither did he. He was finding he had to pull his belt tighter to keep his pants from slipping down, making them look and feel baggy. His shirts felt tighter around his shoulders and chest. When he looked in the mirror to shave, it was as if he was looking at someone else, like a more fit twin. He was still half asleep when he showered and shaved, and that's the way it had been every morning for the past few months.

"You have been working out," exclaimed Marilee, "Have you been going to the gym? You look fabulous."

"I guess I have," said a confounded Dante who was guessing somehow, he had, but couldn't remember when. He wondered if he was some sort of split personality; someone who became someone else and headed off to the gym each night. There was a faint recollection of engaging in tough physical activity, but it was in a gym unlike any he could remember having seen in this neighborhood.

"Sorry," he said as he wiped a droplet of drool from the corner of his mouth with his sleeve, "I don't know what is going on and I am so exhausted. And strange things have been happening to me."

"I had all that muscle pain a few weeks back. As that cleared, I sprained my ankle. I don't know how. Today I wake up with a knife cut on my hand someone, I don't know who, but definitely not a nurse or doctor, has bandaged."

He undid the bandage to show her. To his shock, what had been a deep cut that morning was now nothing more than a pinkish line across his palm. Marilee couldn't resist, "Are you seeing someone?"

"I don't know, maybe," responded a bewildered Dante. "I have brief visions of a beautiful woman dancing around me, but not that kind of relationship. She is like my mentor."

As he spoke, his recollection grew a touch clearer. "It's like she's training me to be a medieval warrior. You know, swords, spears, bows and arrows and such."

"Can't say I do," she said, looking beyond him toward the elevators. "Oh, the boys are back. Gotta go. Talk to you later," and she walked off back to her part of the office, disappearing behind her cubby wall.

"Sure, looks like you were working through lunch," said Earl in a loud voice.

"We just spoke for a moment," said Dante in a defensive tone.

"Of course, you did," grinned Earl.

"Give the guy a break, Earl," said Adam.

He turned to Dante, a serious expression on his face. "I know how you feel about sports, pal, but our slow pitch season is starting a week next Friday right after work. We only have eleven players since Korinsky, and Janice left the firm. I hate to ask, but do you think you could come on the team as a backup? You wouldn't have to play unless someone got hurt or couldn't make the game."

Adam was used to Dante making excuses before outright refusal. To his amazement Dante, with no hesitation, said, "sure."

"Really!" exclaimed Adam.

"Why not," said Dante.

Adam turned towards the general office area. "Hey everybody," he called out, "Good news, Dante is joining slow pitch."

Participants and regular spectators, which meant most of the staff, applauded at the news. It didn't matter if a new, non-player joined the team. They tended to be among the weaker teams in the mercantile league, anyway. They felt having Dante join the team completed things.

Chapter 15. The Boy Can Play

Opening day of the slow pitch league and everyone from Dante, Adam and Earl's office were at the game. Some, including Dante, were on the edge of the field beside the enclosure with the benches and the equipment bags called the dugout. Dante, not having spent anytime following sports, didn't know why.

The office crowd seated in the stands were boisterous and loud even before the game began. For them, the game was always a laugh, but the after-game celebration at a local pub was more intriguing. During the game they would cheer. The team members would play their hearts out and still lose, then they would all go off for a rousing evening of drinks, finger food, and fun.

Dante sat at the end of the bench and twiddled his thumbs. The first inning passed with his office team, The Motley Adders, behind three to nothing. The next two innings saw the Adders out scored four to nothing. An astonished Adam could not believe his eyes seeing his non-competitive friend up from the bench and leaning against the cage shouting, "Come on, hitter, come on Jack, hit that ball."

Dante's encouragement worked and Jack the mail boy and the team's best athlete, contacted the ball rolling it through the gap, making it to second base before the surprised shortstop could gather it up and throw it to the second baseman. The next hitter struck out. Then it was Marilee's turn at bat. She beat out a single, letting Jack make it over to third. Then disaster struck. Earl's secretary, Mary, was to be next up. She was beside the dugout taking some practice swings when she slipped on a ball that hadn't made it into the equipment bag after the warmup.

It wasn't a serious injury, but Mary would not be able to run the bases if she was to get a lucky hit. Adam called time out and looked around for someone to take her place. He couldn't believe what he saw. Dante was pointing at himself. Adam couldn't hear him over the din, but it looked like he was asking to be put in the game. Adam signaled him to come.

While Adam met with the umpire to insert the substitution, Dante took two practice swings. "Ok, you're up, but you know it means you're in for the rest of the game," Adam informed him as he returned from talking with the Umpire.

Dante shrugged and walked up to the plate. Imitating the other hitters, he held the bat off his shoulder. It wasn't the perfect stance, by far, but he looked ready. The crowd from Dante's office had been silent as two of her fellow players helped Mary off the field and into the stands, and Dante made his way to the plate. Then the noise resumed, the chanting, the shouting, and the laughter.

The first pitch was slow and wide. Dante was sure he could have gotten there and hit it, but he had seen enough games to know you let those go by. The next pitch came right down the middle. To Dante's mind, it seemed to be taking an inordinate amount of time to get to him. It was hard, but he was patient. When it, at last, reached him, he swung the bat as Astrada had taught him, although he didn't remember the lesson. Meet the opponent with full strength and follow through to a quick, maximum extension. The bat contacted the ball with a crisp smack.

Everyone froze in amazement as they watched the ball soar through the air, over the outfield fence, and disappear among the trees off in the distance. At the crack of the bat, Jack scurried for home. With Adam shouting directions, Dante walked around the bases, Marilee a base ahead of him, until he was back at home plate.

Everyone in the dugout had come out to greet Dante as he made his way back. They were congratulating him, patting him on the back, shaking his hand. The score was now seven to three as Earl stepped up to the plate. The other team, still stunned by Dante's colossal hit, were not yet ready when Earl hit the ball to the far-right corner of the field. With the opposition's concentration still focused on the disappearing ball off Dante's bat, the outfielder failed to react fast enough, allowing Earl to follow Dante's home run with one of his own. While nowhere near as spectacular as Dante's, it made it seven to four on the score board.

A pop up and a strike out later, the Adders were headed for the field. Dante replaced Mary in right field, her glove which he had to borrow was a little tight on his hand. Adam's pitching, while not the greatest, was the best the Adders could muster. The opposition, now back in focus, were ready. Dante watched as the opposing teams batter hit Adam's first pitch cleanly and it looped just overhead of the shortstop to land midfield. Dante wondered why no one caught it. Although it wasn't his responsibility, Dante knew he could have.

The next hit was a hard line drive right up the center. Rather than worrying about the center fielder catching it,

Dante bolted across the field and hauled it out of the air. He then threw it to Marilee at third base, tagging out the runner.

Not everyone had seen the play, but those who did were gasping in amazement. This was an apocryphal story that would make the rounds of the office for years. The umpire called Adam over to him. "You know it's against the rules to have an 'A' league player or above on your roster," he said, "and that guy looks like at least a Triple-A guy to me."

"Honestly," returned Adam, "I know for a fact that guy has never played any kind of baseball, or any other sport in his entire life, and I've known him since elementary school. It's gotta be a real fluke, beginner's luck."

It was neither a fluke nor luck as Dante continued his stupendous play over the next three innings. He hit two more home runs, both with players on base, and made several stupendous catches from his right field position. The final score was nine, eight for the Adders. It was their first win in three years. Both the team members and the spectators from the office went wild. The after celebration at the pub was unmatched. Everyone was cheering Dante, buying him drinks, grabbing him by the arm and telling him how amazing he was.

The evening's joy was unprecedented and when it ended, more cabs, Ubers and Lyfts were called than ever before. It was a fabulous and unexpected opening day and opening day celebration for the Motley Adders and their fans. Despite free drinks, however, Dante felt tired, but not drunk when he entered his apartment. He went to the bathroom and then straight to bed.

As he sat up on the pallet in the Stade Arcanium, Astrada holding out a crossbow for him, all he could think was, "Thank God tomorrow is Saturday."

Chapter 16. Where

After the Motley Adders won their second game, thanks to Dante's exceptional hitting and marvelous fielding, there were a number of complaints made to the governing body of the mercantile slo-pitch league. They accused the Adders of bringing a ringer onto their team. The league governors called Adam, the coach and manager of the team, for a meeting. Somehow, he convinced them Dante had never played a sport before in his life and while he might be a natural; he wasn't a ringer.

They approved Dante to play but, although no one uttered it out loud, with some restrictions. Against his will, Adam had to tell his friend to tone it down on the field; take a little off the swing and stick to playing defense in his own position. Sensing it might be difficult for Dante to hold back, Adam penciled him in at third base and told him to stay on the left side of the field and let Jack and Earl and Marilee play their own areas. If they booted the ball sometimes, not to worry because the more work they got, the better they would be.

Dante, whose nights were spent being trained to always go hard, to keep improving, to compete to win, found it difficult to restrain himself on the field, but he did. Still, his presence lifted the spirit of the team and made them want to work harder. They won their share of games and were never out of one. It was looking as if they might make the playoffs.

When Adam came back with the official word Dante could play, Earl chipped in to say Dante needed a better glove. Mary's glove was not the best quality, and it was tight on his hand. Since Mary stilled played, she needed a glove that fit, not one stretched and ripped by the hand of the team ace. "I think I have an old one at home," offered Adam.

"Hey, come on," said Earl, "Dante has a damn good salary. He can afford to get his own glove."

Dante thought it made sense and agreed that after work the next day, the three of them would go to a local sporting goods store and help him decide on a decent glove.

Shopping with Adam and Earl was always a challenge for Dante. This trip was no exception. This store sold some more exotic sports paraphernalia and Earl got excited. When this happened, he would turn into a twelve-year-old. He handled everything from rugby cleats, to target pistols, hockey sticks, bats, expensive golf clubs. The sight of a display showing a crossbow grabbed his adolescent attention. He took it from a mannikin's hand and aimed it at his friends.

This made them uncomfortable, and they both hurried to step aside and away from the line of fire just as a clerk was coming to ask Earl to please put it back. Earl, unaware that someone had set the bolt and cocked it, to add more realism to the display or because they, like Earl, were foolish, squeezed the release. There was a twang, and the bolt launched itself on a deadly path towards the approaching salesclerk.

Dante, having been told by Astrada never to take his eyes off a weapon being pointed in his direction, had. without thinking, focused in on the business end of the bow. The bolt came fast, but for him it seemed to slow down as it was about to shoot past him. He reached out and grabbed it by the shaft. It was shorter than the bolts he had trained on, but he was easily able to catch it, his grasp stopping it in mid-flight. He didn't know how he could do this, but from the moment Earl picked up the bow, he knew he could.

Adam gasped, the clerk cringed, and Earl yelled, "Holy shit. I didn't know it was loaded."

"How the hell did you do that?" demanded Adam.

"Yeah, Jeez, thank you," said the clerk, his voice trembling, "I think it was coming straight for me."

"Yeah, it was," said Dante.

Like a foul-mouthed mother, Adam shouted at Earl, to put that god damned thing down and get the fuck over here and apologize to the clerk and thank Dante for saving your effing bacon. He turned back to Dante and repeated, "How the hell did you do that?" adding, "I heard the release, but I couldn't even see the bolt it was moving too fast and," he shook his head in disbelief, "you just reached out and caught it."

"Like you were reaching for a pop fly or picking up a pencil at your desk. Where, on earth, did you learn to do that?"

Dante with a slight tilt of his head said, "Not on this earth, that's for sure."

He knew it sounded stupid to say, but somehow it felt like it was true. "I just saw it coming, all the way. Couldn't you guys see it?"

Somehow, he realized they couldn't. "Let's get out of here," said Adam and started towards the door.

Dante put a hand on the clerk's shoulder. He was still trembling. "You okay?" he asked.

The clerk shook his head in a weak affirmative. All he could say was, "Thank you. You might have saved my life."

He started to shake, "Oh God, I have to sit down, I might have been killed. Thank you, thank you, thank you."

The clerk was still shaking and thanking Dante as the three friends left the shop. "Honest to God, guys, I didn't know they loaded it," said Earl who was shaking as hard as the store clerk. "I did it again, didn't I, Dante? And you saved me again, didn't you? Thank god for a friend like you."

"Forget it," said Dante, patting Earl on the back.

Dante knew he shouldn't be telling Earl to forget his foolishness. He should shout at him, telling him to think before he acted, to watch what he was doing and be more careful, but he didn't want to think about any of that. Something was going on with him and it was something he didn't want to think about or even know about. The changes he was seeing in himself terrified him. It was as if he was becoming someone else, someone he didn't recognize. He was sleeker, stronger, more observant, faster, all outstanding qualities, he had to admit, but he wasn't sure he liked any of it.

Despite his parents being over-protective to a fault, they loved him and had provided him with a comfortable life. He had learned to like who he was, an average guy living an average life. Average guys didn't move the way he could on the ball field. They didn't catch crossbow bolts in flight with their bare hands.

That night when he lay on his bed and found himself on the pallet in the Stade Arcanium, he had to ask the question. What is happening to me and why?

Astrada thought the answer was a simple one. "You are learning to be a warrior. You are growing stronger and more skillful. And you are doing it because we need you."

That was OK, Dante figured, but it didn't answer his question. What he really wanted to know was when he became this champion, he was told he was destined to be, would he still be Dante? Would he still be Adam and Earl's friend, a good boss at work and perhaps even become a little closer, hell, maybe a lot closer with Marilee. No one could answer any of those questions for him. Tauren and Astrada would be more concerned why he felt a reluctance about taking on the role they said was his, earth's champion. His friends, who knew him well, might agree.

Chapter 17. Conquering

Unlike earth and the other planets bearing sentient life in a variety of dimensions, there was no clear north or south, hence no east or west in purgatory. Each domain instituted its own. The Grand Dukes much earlier than Davlos or Fluglaz had to decide how to name directions. For them, the regal sedes, the duke's throne, was the center of the world.

When the Duke sat, his brandished sword was in his right. It became the direction, sword. He held his dagger with his left hand. It became the direction, dagger. When standing or when at peace and walking, his shield rested against his back. So, the direction behind him as he sat was shield and the direction in front, they called greaves for the piece of armor covering his shins. Over time, they had reduced it all to "ord, dak, shye, and gree."

The older domains of purgatory were found to the dak and to the shye. Their home worlds, even their universes in some cases, had long since collapsed and separated into clouds of the various elements that had once fostered life. Some other domains in these directions were little more than neglected remnants of once rich and ingenious societies. They were now either empty altogether or sparsely populated with a few whose time of atonement wasn't yet done.

To the ord and the gree were the purgatorial domains of the newer worlds, the still vibrant universes, and dimensions. Fluglaz sent armies in each direction. Domains to the dak and shye offered little resistance to the invaders. For the most part, the domains to the ord and gree made every attempt to defend their borders against incursion. Sometimes these defenses were more for show than real as Fluglaz, or his deputies had already bought off the corrupted guardians. In other cases, the defense would be intense, but few domains had well trained champions to lead them along. Fluglaz' armies were strong in numbers, the warriors brutal and unbending. Few domain defenses could last long against them.

The vast array of warriors in Fluglaz's invasion forces were all first lifers. They were not in purgatory seeking atonement, and they had no desire to die. Most domains didn't have anywhere near the numbers of first lifers Fluglaz's associated domains did, and many first lifers feeling threatened by Fluglaz's invading legions fled back to their living world before they arrived. Others remained joined with the atoners or second lifers to help, but their numbers were inadequate against Fluglaz's legions.

The atoners were less resistance to the possibility of death. If killed, they knew they would be reanimated and returned their beginning point. The nature of their existence constrained them from leaving their domain. They might fight to protect their present homeland, but their primary purpose was to seek atonement. For many, the persecution and disruption included in alien domination was just another aspect of it.

With Astrada and Tauren and the stories of the champion, the first life population of earth's purgatory, had decided they were prepared to face down any invasion. While not so populous a group as the first lifers of Fluglaz's domain, they were the closest match to his warriors, and they were training hard. Astrada had full knowledge of the warrior training Davlos, and his predecessors went through. She also knew that Fluglaz was by nature too bloodthirsty and combative to have his warriors learn the fine points of combat. She was not.

Earth's purgatory was many domains distant ord of Fluglaz's duchy. It was said to be an exceptional domain. Its beautiful metropolis with its stately buildings covered billions of hectares. Outside the vast city, it was well organized and fruitful. Even more fascinating, especially to a geographer, was that its land mass was undergoing rapid expansion along with the growing population on earth.

Fluglaz was determined to add it to his retinue of domains. Ruling that much of purgatory would mean controlling an empire, enormous beyond imagining. He could see himself exchanging the title of Grand Duke for the title of Emperor. This vision, like his lust for power, was irresistible.

Tauren was aware Fluglaz armies, having conquered those many domains separating earth's from Fluglaz and his place, would soon be at the border. Fluglaz might even make his way to join with his armies in the ord. This would be his greatest conquest since he had stepped in to take the place of Davlos. From there he believed he could go on to conquer more domains, ultimately gathering all of purgatory under his rule. This was Fluglaz hubris. To conquer and control all was only an illusion for the great and ever expanding plain of purgatory stretched to infinity in all directions.

Meanwhile, Fluglaz, in his vanity, was prepared to sacrifice vast numbers of first lifers both in his armies and in the many domains he invaded. Unlike the Grand Dukes before him, he had no interest in protecting and preserving the first lifers even of his own society. His ambition was all encompassing and those who would die in battle for his greater glory meant nothing to him.

For Tauren, this was the worst aspect of the invasion of earth's domain. The countless lives that would be lost. Oh yes, they would return to their own domains, now as atonement seekers, but such a waste of first life. Still, he knew with absolute clarity this bloodthirsty encounter would happen and it was essential he and his champion, Astrada and all the others, needed to do everything they could to protect their realm from the cold brutality of Duke Fluglaz.

Tauren delighted to see Astrada was doing her work well. Earth's champion was looking like a champion. While the more timid of the first lifers had fled back to the earth, most remained, eager to follow Tauren, Astrada and their champion into battle. It saddened Tauren to think it had come to this. He admired their courage, but come victory or defeat, it would try their metal.

Dante had come a long way from the flabby out of shape person who first dropped through the portal of his bed. With Astrada around, however, he never felt that way at the Stade Arcanium. If he believed Astrada, he was weak, his skill mediocre, and his personality uninspiring. Although she would never admit it to him, she was both proud of the work she had done to turn Dante into a champion and pleased with his success.

It was only back among his friends, companions and fellow workers on earth Dante got any props for what he had become.

Chapter 18. Real

As summer stretched on towards fall, Dante's life was never dull. He was leading his Office Slo-pitch team into the playoffs with his stellar play and motivated by his success, the vastly improved play of those around him. There were barbecues to attend, and he didn't miss any of them. Often, he would arrive with a case of beer and several large steaks. Since there was always lots of food, Marilee might have been the only one to notice just how hungry Dante was. In previous years, he never went back for seconds.

The barbecues and pool parties were another thing. For many years Dante had been a reluctant participant. He would come but was far too shy to bring a bathing suit; he couldn't swim, and his dumpy appearance embarrassed him. Even as the new Dante, he was still shy to don a bathing suit, but it was no longer because he was too dumpy. Now before heading off to a pool party, he would check himself in the mirror and there was no question about it, he was ripped. Dante was just as embarrassed by his rippling muscles, his broad shoulders, and his body builder's pecs.

As for swimming, his confidence there had changed. He no longer avoided the water out of fear of drowning. It was a pervasive fear drummed into him by his parents. They had made it quite clear; swimming was far too dangerous and even lessons were out of the question. He didn't know how he was so certain, but he knew he was an excellent swimmer. What he didn't remember was Astrada, and some of her fellow instructors had taught him that skill in the large waterways and pools beside the Stade Arcanium.

Confirmation of his competence with this skill came one weekend at an office group beach party. While it was a beautiful day, the lake was rough. They had to cook in shelters, and all were advised not to go into the deep water. The teenage son of one of the company's directors didn't believe this advisory included him. He had brought a canoe and was determined he was going to get out on the lake in it.

Almost everyone was in the cooking shelter out of the wind. The conversation and the laughter were loud. The crashing of the waves, the wind rustling through the trees and the delicious smells of cooking made the group more boisterous than usual, and truth be told, they were a boisterous group to begin with. No one noticed the young man launch his canoe and make his way against the waves away from the shore and the happy celebrants.

Everything was fine until the canoeist decided that he had gone out far enough and it was time to turn it around and return to shore. He carelessly turned the canoe broadside to the waves just as a gust picked up, sending an immense wave crashing into the canoe's side and flipping it. The young man let out a cry for help as he tumbled into the water. Despite all the noise, Dante heard him and stepped out of the cooking shelter to see where the call had come from.

He saw the canoe bobbing upright in the waves, and the head of the director's son in the swell beside it. He watched as the canoe banged against the young man's head and knew right away, he was in trouble. Pulling off his shirt and tossing the contents of his pocket onto the nearest picnic table, Dante raced to the water. Within moments, he was swimming fiercely toward the floundering young man. His strokes were smooth and clean and watching the quickness and power of his stroke amazed all those who had left the cook shelter to see what the fuss was.

The canoeist was close to six hundred meters from the shore and unconscious from striking his head on the hard wood of the canoe's gunwale. Frothy whitecaps stormed towards him. The waves were about to impact the canoe, striking the boy again as it turned into the waves and leapt away from him. Dante reached him just in time. Taking hold of the dazed young man with one arm, he began swimming back to shore. The spectators were so overwhelmed by what they saw, for a moment they froze. Then everyone seemed to move as one. The better swimmers raced out to meet Dante and once he could stand, took hold of the young man, and brought him to shore.

Some others went off to get the canoe while a few went to find the first aid kit. Apart from a bump on his head the size of a turnip, the young canoeist was fortunate he had not been more seriously injured. He did take in a lot of water, and it took a moment or two of heavy coughing to clear. He staggered to his feet and trying to assure everyone he was alright, although they could see he was still a little foggy about what had happened.

The director had watched in horror as the rescue took place. He ran over to Dante and grasped him by the shoulder. He reached out to shake Dante's hand, his gratefulness obvious. "Wow, were you a professional swimmer?" asked one of the newer interns.

The ones who had known Dante for years were wondering who this guy really was. "What the hell did you do with my friend Dante, anyway?" demanded Earl.

What Earl and the others didn't realize, Dante was asking himself the same question and he could come up with no better conclusion than theirs. They may believe he was working out or busy training, although if they thought about it, they would recognize as Dante did, how this wasn't possible. There were no fitness centers open all night, the only time Dante could do that. Any other time there was almost always someone around him or in touch with him by phone or computer.

It was only in retrospect that Dante could really realize what he had done out on the lake. It was not only that he could swim out and rescue the boy; it was also the speed and power he had possessed as he raced toward the floundering youth. While racing to rescue the boy, he had given no thought to his swimming or to the treacherous conditions around him. His only goal was to save the young man. It was only in retrospect he understood he accomplished something that in the past would have terrified him and yet, through it all, he had felt no fear. How was it even possible he could do such a thing?

It wasn't until night as he slipped through the portal into the Stade Arcanium, he understood what was happening to him. Astrada had trained him and even now she still scared the hell out of him, but while she was fierce, she was a very skilled coach. Her fierce aggression and the efforts of her fellow trainers on the field forced him to face his immediate fear and forget the rest as he got down to business. Thinking about this later, he began to see how much his empathy and wish to protect his fellows had grown and how ready he was to put those feelings into action. He was coming to realize the role of earth's champion was much more than being a skilled warrior.

Along with this growing awareness, Dante's focus and concentration sharpened. He was not developing his skills for Tauren or Astrada, but for all humanity, for Adam and Earl, and Marilee, and the director's son, and everyone else he knew or came in contact with as well as every single human on earth and in purgatory, living or dead. He could feel the weight of the responsibility, but oddly enough, it didn't seem a burden.

Returning to his daily life, Dante pushed this knowledge from his conscious mind, but in his subconscious, it was flowering.

Chapter 19. Plans

Tauren and Astrada could both see Dante was progressing towards his destiny. In any form of battle, with or without weapons, Dante was proving himself superior not only to his fellow trainees but also to the instructors. Astrada was one of the few who could still stand toe to toe with him. As the exchanges grew more intense, Astrada could see it was only a matter of time before the student, as between her and Davlos, would surpass the master.

Back in the daily world, Dante knew he was growing more powerful, more agile, his mind keener and more observant. His thoughts were quicker and his decision making more precise. Knowing this was happening without knowing why bothered him. While at some level he knew it made sense, at a conscious level he couldn't understand any of it. All he knew was it was affecting his everyday life. He was getting far too much respect from his co-workers, and it was getting to where he was feeling more isolated.

He wasn't the beloved supervisor of his department anymore; he was the idol. The others no longer turned to him for support with their work problems. When they approached him, it was to seek out his definitive word on some key issue or other. Working together with staff members, something Dante had loved to do, no longer occurred. Staff seemed shy of him, careful and respectful. There was no shared laughter as there had been before. Even Adam and Earl deferred to him, and

Marilee tiptoed around him. Although they liked Dante, the office staff was hesitant to invite him to their social events. If they invited him, they treated him like royalty, serving him, not letting him do things on his own. He didn't want to be royalty; he wanted to be one of the gang.

No one in the company Dante worked for could deny his department had reached new levels of efficiency and was the most successful. This didn't go unnoticed by the upper administration. The director whose son Dante saved had been following his work for some time and was pushing the directorship to consider him for a significant promotion. He felt Dante had what it took to join senior management, and most of the other directors on studying Dante's progress within his department were falling in line with this thinking.

An assistant director's position would be opening soon in a distant office. The directors agreed Dante would be perfect for it. The Chief Executive was willing to listen to the opinions of the directors and looked into Dante's work record. Soon after that, the directors' choice for assistant director was approved. The directors given permission to meet with Dante and offer him the position. This procedure was rare. In most cases senior managers were offered the directorships, or the firm gave the position to someone brought in from another company. Dante's profile was rich enough they could bypass the usual procedure and offer him the position.

There was to be a general meeting of all financial staff in two weeks. The directors and senior executives would be there. The directors decided it would be an excellent time to bring Dante in, interview him, and then offer him the position. Until then, Dante could continue to do his work in blissful ignorance. Love the way directors of big companies work!

During the working day, Dante felt very uncomfortable as his coworkers' behavior towards him had changed so much. This was very difficult for him, and he wasn't sure why it happened. He still had no significant memory of his nights in purgatory. Except for brief and indeterminate flashes, his day life and his nights of training were two worlds that didn't meet.

While on the training court in Purgatory, Dante realized the separation of his nighttime activities from his daytime ones, was not a bad thing. Had he remembered the odd reality of his nights, and said something, he would most likely have been locked away or at least in treatment with a variety of medical and psychological professionals. This dichotomous lifestyle had been going on for a long time, and he was reaching a level of comfort with the reality of its odd and mysterious aspects. Aware of this, he still sought out Tauren to ask if he could be permitted to remember his training and purgatory the next day.

Without hesitation, Tauren informed him there was not the slightest chance that would happen before the time was right. He could have added the time might never be right. Tauren knew if anything about his nights slipped out, people would think he was crazy, and it would be more complicated if he had to withdraw his champion from a psychiatric ward. In the end, what Dante needed to remember was not dependent on Tauren, but on Fluglaz, or some other hostile who might bring war across the boundary of earth's part of purgatory. Although it irked Dante, this was the case, he accepted it. He wouldn't remember in the morning, anyway.

He had grown more comfortable in his role, and his curiosity blossomed. During a brief rest from his intensive training, sitting between Astrada and Tauren, he decided he wanted to know more about the domain for which he was champion. "So," he asked to neither one in particular, "If this is the place where those who have died back in the world come to atone and wait to be taken to their ultimate reward, could I visit my grandfather? I only met him once, but he seemed like a nice man."

"How many centuries do you have?" Grinned Tauren, "There are so many things to consider. To begin with, you would have known your grandfather as an older man. He would appear much younger here. Another thing, purgatory keeps expanding with a population of many trillions, and those who waken in purgatory can be much like you when you return to earth. Their specific memories of the lives they lived are vague and uncertain. Often, they only remember what they needed to atone for"

Tauren told him that very few souls were carried off by angels or demons, so the population grew continuously. "You're telling me few souls get taken to their ultimate reward or punishment. I thought for many, the time would be short."

"Well," replied Tauren, "atonement appears to be a long and arduous task for most and to tell you the truth, just because one goes into either the darkness or the light doesn't necessarily mean ultimate reward or final punishment. We really don't know."

"Don't look at me," said Astrada, "Nearly everyone was a living being where I was. They had staked out a domain for the living and it was large."

"You mean they pushed the atoners away?" Dante asked.

"I believe the worlds that part of purgatory served were old, and many had long since been deserted. So, while still in the billions, they were far fewer than here. Purgatory, it seems, only expands, it doesn't shrink. Ok, let's get back to it. weapons drill!"

Assuming the stance, Dante had a brief vision. He saw thousands of people crowding the edges of the city and off into the countryside. They were dressed in many styles, ancient and modern. Most seemed to be neither particularly young nor old. He could see them interacting and sensed that only a part of their personality participated in social activity. One could sense some were more, and some were less deep in introspection. He understood they were alone with their thoughts, deep in a personal solitude, yet still aware and participants in their immediate world. They were part the person they had been and part the person they wanted to be. The vision vanished in an instant as Astrada, without an "en garde" lunged toward him, blade extended. He swept his blade up to parry her thrust and she was back at him again.

Chapter 20. Rather

The activity in the office, in fact, throughout the building was frenzied. It was as if life slipped into fourth gear and the foot pressed down hard on the accelerator. It was a big week coming up for the entire firm. Executives from across the country and around the world were coming in for the annual meeting. Not only were there a massive number of work goals, but also, they were making preparations for the big meetings about to take place. There seemed to be more coming this year than ever before. Each arriving executive needed to be welcomed. It seemed like office tours were occurring every few minutes as new arrivals for the meetings showed up.

Much to his chagrin, Dante found himself one of the centrepieces of these executive tours. It was hard to get any work done when every few minutes he was being introduced to some senior director, district coordinator, or vice president. This hadn't happened to him any other time the senior administrators met.

He recognized the director who brought most of the visitors to his tiny office. It was the father of the boy he saved from the canoe misadventure. Perhaps this was his way of saying thanks, or perhaps he was now aware of Dante, never having been before. The one time the director came to visit Dante's desk with another of the senior executives, he was about to ask if he could tone it down so he could spend more time helping his staff. Instead, the director asked Dante to join him and the vice president of resource in one of the smaller conference rooms on the tip floor.

The request overawed Dante. The VP accompanying the director was one of the most senior in the company. The president was an illusory figure around the building, this VP was not. Everybody deemed him as the 'master of the house.' Had he done something wrong? Although he racked his brain on the elevator ride, he couldn't think of what he might have done to have messed up enough to have to meet with the 'master.'

It was all very cordial as they offered Dante one of the comfortable looking executive chairs to sit in. It was, he discovered, just as comfortable as it looked. He swallowed hard as the two senior executives sat and the VP flipped through some papers in a thick folder. "Your work for us has been excellent, top notch. I want you to know everyone on the top floor is impressed."

Dante was about to thank him when he cut off any opportunity by adding, "We all feel you are a key member of this firm, and we all believe that such excellent work should not go unrewarded."

"Wow," thought Dante, "Maybe I'm getting a raise."

The VP continued, "Your kind of competence and effort is what made this company what it is today, and we would like to offer you an assistant director's portfolio. There is a position opening up in our Vancouver office soon and we would like to send you there to take it over the."

Dante's jaw dropped. "Think it over, young man. I know it is a lot to take in. The position is there for you in the middle of this month. That would give you a few days to wrap up here and make your way out west. Don't worry about a place to stay. We will cover it until you are settled."

"You don't have to answer right away. I'm sure it is a surprise. You know we rarely choose our directorship this way."

With smiles and back pats, the master and the VPs dismissed him, allowing a bemused Dante to go back to his office. He was useless for the rest of the day. His staff could see his mind was elsewhere and left him alone. The director visited Dante one more time, accompanied by a rather austere looking gentleman, whose greying hair and sharp beardless chin made him look as he may have been a leading man in movies not too long back. "Dante," said the director, "This is Joseph Mantacore, he is vice president and chief executive officer of the Vancouver branch."

"Sir," was all Dante could say.

"Nice to meet you, young man. May I call you Dante?" said Mantacore as he extended his hand, "looking forward to working with you. Heard good things."

"Thank you, sir!" Replied Dante.

The conversation was cut short as the Vancouver Chief looked at his watch and exclaimed, "My gosh, gotta run, I have a dinner date with my daughter at four."

Looking back as he hurried out the door, he half waved at Dante, "Nice to meet you. Hope to be seeing you soon."

He was out the door before Dante could get out anything more than, "Nice meeting you, too, sir."

Dante's head was spinning as he made his way home. He said nothing to Adam, Earl or Marilee and had left on his own.

"NOT A CHANCE," SAID Tauren, "We can't have you working on your champion's skills and feeling your way around a new job in a new city at the same time. Add to it, the hassle of building a new portal, although that's the least of it."

Dante was not so certain. As he had changed, things around him seemed to have changed, too. His sense was that among his staff and with office friends, he was being pushed to the side. They might have seen him through fresh eyes and were reluctant to impose on him, but he didn't see that. In his mind, he was still the same person, just more physically fit.

He could have excused his friends and staffers from not dropping by. The impending general meetings made everyone much busier than usual, but this avoidance of him had been going on for more than a month. Marilee hadn't even come by his desk in over three weeks, and Adam and Earl's visits had slowed right down. If no-one wanted to hang out with him or ask him to join them when they socialized, then a move to Vancouver would at least increase his income and perhaps let him make some new friends, friends who wouldn't desert him for no known reason.

Now Dante found himself torn. It was not so much between his friends and coworkers and a new job, as a director, in Vancouver, but between that and Tauren's vaguely remembered urging to turn it down. He wondered why he felt the disconnect. Something was urging him to turn down the plummy promotion and stay where he was, but he didn't know what that something was. There wasn't a sense this had anything to do with leaving his friends, but he latched on to the idea it was. It was only when he was back in the training grounds of purgatory, he understood the source of his inner conflict. Back on the job, it once again became all about leaving his now distant friends behind.

In either place, the decision was overwhelming him. It was easier to duel with Astrada and the others than spend any time thinking about the choice he would soon have to make. Astrada couldn't help but be impressed by the energy he put into his personal combat training. When he was like that, she was one of the very few who could stand with him. The rest were busy with icepacks nursing their aches and pains.

Chapter 21. Almost

Duke Fluglaz was savoring his role as conqueror, and it was sweet. His armies had taken possession of the surrounding domains and were reaching farther afield. The domains he now controlled were ancient ones, and most of the living who had n time past come through the portals were as ancient as the cultures they represented and few in numbers. Those reborn to atonement in these domains were, by purgatory's standards, even fewer.

Most of the conquered domains being ancient, lacked vitality. They were neglected. Many of the buildings in their vast cities had fallen into disrepair. While it opened more area for the Fluglaz's subjects to move into, it didn't satisfy him. He sought to rule domains brimming with vitality, domains where those atoning could still sustain a culture of growth. Directions were meaningless and mainly arbitrary in purgatory. The younger domains were out there drawing the conqueror and his armies towards Earth's domain.

Time does not operate the same in purgatory as in the worlds of the living. Fluglaz's path of conquest and its arrival at earth's domain was both imminent and distant. Each domain his forces easily conquered required he and his senior officers find and ensconce some useful puppets in positions of power, assign one of his officers to serve as governor, and provide him with a sizeable militia. This may have slowed the thrust of Fluglaz's ambitions, but with each new conquest, it only encouraged him.

In most instances, there had been little or no resistance. He was not happy. Easy conquest did not appeal to his blood thirsty, vicious nature. He sent advance groups out to find the easiest domains to claim and had them do so on his behalf. These warrior cadres were large enough to subdue many domains, and capable of overthrowing most others. Like their duke, they were brutal, ferocious beings, fierce fighters and remorseless.

One of these squadrons was making its way towards earth's domain. One domain they were passing through was experiencing chaos in their part of the multiverse. War and galactic level disaster were exploding the numbers of those reborn to atonement. The domain was expanding at a rapid rate as Fluglaz's squadron was making its way to its outer limits. They had subdued the living refugees and taken control of the domain with little effort. They left a governor and a small group of their fellows to make sure their balance of power was kept. Four more were ordered to return to their home domain to inform their Duke of the success. The rest, like Alexander's Legion, still plentiful in numbers, pressed on towards earth's domain.

The expansion of the domain through which they passed delayed their exit. After each night's encampment, the boundaries had been moved farther. What should have taken a short time was now stretching out into a much longer delay. Earth's domain continued to grow without infringing on the domain where Fluglaz's forces found their exit delayed. That part of purgatory was undergoing exponential growth. The delay was a bonus for earth's purgatory as its champion was very near ready. Soon he'd be waking up with all knowledge of who he was and where he had been.

This didn't trouble Dante while he was in purgatory. His training continued to be taxing and intense. There was little time to think about it. Tauren had some concern. He was aware Dante worried about his worldly relationships and confused about his extreme physical and mental capabilities among his peers. Would it help for him to join with his friends knowing the fullness of his status and his power?

While this might be a worry for Tauren, it was of the utmost importance for Dante who would one day return to the earthly plane with full knowledge. This was inevitable because it was from the living earth, he would have to recruit followers. Only the living could provide an adequate defense of the boundaries of earthly purgatory. The atoners could help, and many were willing, but they could never invest fully in it. Only living beings could bring that kind of focus.

While in the realm of purgatory, Dante understood the value of developing his physical strength, his speed and dexterity. Dante had learned extreme hand to hand combat of every sort and had become an expert with about every weapon one could name. He was so busy training and Astrada was such a fierce taskmaster; he didn't have time to meditate on his purpose in doing all this.

Over time Dante understood he had a specific and important role in defending earth's purgatory and by extension earth itself. He knew that alien warriors were approaching, intent on conquest. Something confused him, however. If these future invaders were from an advanced civilization, why was his training focused on such archaic weapons. It was a question he put to Tauren when he had mastered them all.

Tauren explained to him concussive weapons did not work in purgatory. Any weapon requiring explosive energy was useless there. Gas powered vehicles would not work as they required minor explosions. Electricity was also limited. Storage batteries would work until their charges ran out and there was no way to recharge. The light from the heavenly circle was enough to provide light for all of purgatory, so it was always daytime. It was never the light of the full sun but was at least as bright as a day with light cloud cover.

Candles or oil lamps provided any needed lighting for indoors and cooking stoves and braziers served for cooking. There was no need for heating. The temperature in purgatory was neither too hot, nor too cold. For the atoners, it went unnoticed, for the living, any extremes in temperature they felt were because of the vagaries of their body. If they stayed too close to a fire, they might feel hot. No one would ever feel cold. The weather, if they could call it such, was always temperate. There was no rain, and any wind was only felt around movement of large things, or when the invisible creatures from either the place of light or the place of darkness were present to bring someone to the next level.

The weapons available to those in purgatory were medieval. Swords and maces, knives and spears, bows and crossbows and any other, slashing, burning, cutting, crushing, or stabbing weapon. Hand grenades could be useful according to Tauren if you could throw them hard enough and accurate enough to hit someone. Otherwise, no boom, pull the pin and nothing happens.

"Well," thought Dante, "I guess that makes sense, purgatory is purgatory."

It was a fact the living had lost none of the vicious streak that led to war and warriors among beings. The atoners, although they might draw arms to join their living brothers in some circumstances, were little inclined to fight or even debate. Earth born atoners would be ready to defend their domain from hostile invasion, but the domain bound them, so they were unable to move beyond its limits. What's more, their mode of battle would always lack aggression as they could only focus on defense.

The limited tactical usefulness of the atoners was the reason purgatory needed champions, living heroes and warriors to carry the brunt of any warfare. They could range beyond the borders of the domain. They could attack or set an ambush. Unlike some other domains of purgatory where there were few of the living, and the majority of those had come seeking refuge and serenity not war. They might provide some defense but could never be very committed warriors.

Sometime soon, Dante would have to recruit an army from earth. Since most people there believed purgatory was a fantasy or a metaphysical place, it would not be an easy task. Tauren had not yet broached the subject with Dante, who returned to his days on earth still unaware of his time in the training compound in purgatory.

Chapter 22. Vancouver

Back to daytime in his room on the world called earth, Dante was uncomfortable. One on hand, things were shutting down while on the other, things were opening up. Having no memory of purgatory and the threats it faced, his daily life revolved around his work and the few activities he took part in. His capabilities may disturb his close friends and associates, but even more so, they surprised and frightened him.

He knew the promotion and Vancouver was looming. In some ways he wanted to go. It would be a vindication of his years of hard work for the company. There were new and interesting challenges to overcome, and providing solutions was one of his strongest abilities. Furthermore, it would allow him to escape and forget the rejection he was feeling from his so-called friends and acquaintances. It could be the start of a new and better life for him.

There was also a deep and undecipherable desire to reject the promotion and stay where he was. His friendships he had built over many years, and he had to admit for most of it they were there for him. Did he even want to leave them all behind? For a long time, he had enjoyed his job, and he liked the community right where he was. To be fair, he wasn't aware how much of what appeared to be rejection as his friends shied away from him was because of the same thing bothering him, his sudden evolution into a superior athlete and physical specimen. If he could accept himself, perhaps they would return to accepting him.

There was something else about the promotion that troubled him. Analyze his thinking as he would, he could not figure out what it was bothering him. Whatever it was, he believed this subconscious doubt might well be the crux of the matter. Unknown to him, Tauren's words while not distinct in his memory still infused his unconscious mind. It was a concern, because the Vancouver position was progressing towards vacancy and soon, he would have to decide.

The company wanted him to accept the promotion. He was a solid worker with a good mind for business and a rare quality of leadership. They expected, and were correct, he would do very well in the position and likely, in very short order, be ready for another promotion. This time it would be a full directorship or even vice presidency. Given the innate ability of earth's champion, it could be a sure thing. At another time, it would be an absolute certainty. Now it rested in the hands of Dante's interior storm and Tauren's powerful influence.

He needed to talk, to be with those who were close to him. His parents had long since moved back to the Midwest. They had gone back to the commune, now a hip farm community where Dante had been born. He could FaceTime, Skype or Zoom them, but it wouldn't be the same. And, anyway, they continued to be overprotective and anything he proposed, they would be certain to disapprove of. For them, anything that might endanger him, even the job he now held, was, to them, too risky. The dream they had shared when he was born had ordered them to protect him. They still felt it intensely.

Perhaps the dream voice could have been clearer about the form this protection should have taken. Dante's parents had taken it literally and if it were possible, would have locked him away from the world. As it was, they hovered like the world's worst helicopter parents preventing him from becoming involved in any physical activity, even walking more than a short distance.

When Dante had left the family home after getting his undergraduate degree and proclaimed his independence, there was little more that they could do but beseech and beg and shed copious tears as they watched him head across the state to graduate school. As for his friends Adam and Earl, although Dante's parents were always polite and affable with them, they may as well have been the devil.

These were his oldest and most loyal friends. If he couldn't count on them, who could he count on? When, that afternoon, he approached Earl and Adam to join him for a drink; they were astonished. He was still their friend, but in so many ways he was far different from the Dante they knew. While their perceptions may have changed, in the most important ways, Dante had not.

They had drawn back from the new and improved Dante, not because of anything he had done, but in deference to someone who seemed to be different from the person they laughed with and teased and shared beers. Perhaps they found it hard to relax with someone who could catch a crossbow bolt in mid-flight, swim out through angry waves to rescue someone falling from a canoe or be courted by the manager of a semipro baseball team. How could such a person spend time with the likes of them, two guys who might do well at some stage in their lives but would never make that jump to the pinnacle Dante seemed to have made?

The bonds of friendship were, in this case, much better established than the fear of disfavor. Their doubts about their own value in relation to their long-time friend didn't disappear, but they accepted his invite with delight. It had been some time since they sat and chatted over an amber pint.

Besides Earl and Adam, Dante would have loved to ask Marilee to join them, but he still felt a twinge of misgiving about the forgotten evening and her cold shoulder afterwards. No matter, he had always shared a solid friendship with Earl and Adam. He found them to be honest and sincere, and he respected that. They would help him with his decision. So it was, after work, the three long time companions made their way to a popular local watering hole where Dante presented them with his dilemma.

Surprised, yet not surprised, the two friends recognized his dilemma. The logic of the company offering him such a promotion made sense. There was no doubt, Dante was leadership material. They also understand his indecision regarding moving to the distant west coast. Neither Adam nor Earl wanted him to go. Losing their best friend was something they didn't want despite their standoffishness of late. Holding him back from something he deserved, was not an option for them either. Both realized he deserved the promotion, but also knew that if he refused, his career would likely stagnate. It made for a long evening of back and forth until the beer buzz was strong enough leading them to slip into their traditional silliness.

Dante stumbled through his door and collapsed on the bed, feeling better than he had in months. He had made a decision and would decline the promotion. Certain as he was, he still couldn't pinpoint the key argument in his choice. Moments later with his arrival in purgatory, he understood. Sitting up on his pallet in the practice grounds of purgatory to face the intensity of Astrada's drills, he felt a slight headache. It was a mild hangover.

Tauren had once told him, beers, and spirits, like explosives, had no effect in Purgatory. There was wine to drink with meals, but without the kick. There were other sources of inebriation, but in earth's domain, few were aware or interested. In other domains, especially among the living residents, they had greater or lesser popularity. This depended on the state of the domain and the particular guardian.

Chapter 23. One Boss

Dante knew the call from head office would come sooner than later, and he had his answer. The offer was appreciated, and he had spent considerable time thinking about it. Right now, he was just not prepared to move. He practiced in front of the mirror, on his way to work, and anytime he had a spare moment alone in his office.

Dante wasn't sure why he believed this was the right decision, but he did. Not that he didn't have a twinge of uncertainty. There was no doubt the promotion would have been a major feather in his cap. The salary it would bring was beyond belief. There was some guilt at turning down such a prestigious offer. The executives would be unhappy with his decision, and so it was unlikely anything else would come down the pipe for him soon, if ever. Still, he was more than satisfied his decision was the right one.

Back in the training fields of purgatory, Tauren was satisfied with Dante's decision. His insistence could only go so far. The final choice had to be Dante's. The champion was not under the command of the guardian. They were in many ways equal. The nature of their responsibilities sometimes coincided, but their roles were different. Tauren would serve with the forces protecting earth's domain, the champion was the war chief. Tauren would do his best to impart all he knew about warfare. Tauren knew that in purgatory, and on earth, Dante, as champion, had no superior, but he had to chuckle; he could see Dante deferred to Astrada as if she was his boss. When battle came, they would be comrades in arms with Dante the unspoken leader.

In the office, Dante felt nothing like a leader. He knew he would soon be on the promotion hot seat, and he would have to present himself in front of the directors and the board chair and turn down their very generous offer. When the call came, Dante made his way to meet with his friends Adam and Earl, and he even invited Marilee to join them for some encouragement before boarding the elevator to the senior administration's floor. He told them what his final decision was and although the three couldn't have been happier; they understood the impact the decision would have on their friend Dante's career. As he made his way to the elevator, Marilee ran over to him and wrapped him in a warm embrace and kissed his cheek.

If Dante's heart had been fluttering before, it now skipped. He returned Marilee's affectionate squeeze and as casually as he could under the circumstances, said, "Ok, I'll see you later. Maybe we could grab a bite to eat, or something."

Marilee just smiled and nodded.

On the elevator, Dante may have had some concern about the directors' response to his answer, but he was thinking more about Marilee's embrace. His thoughts as the elevator doors opened on the executive floor were so confused, he turned the wrong way, not realizing it until he came to the doors of the executive washroom.

It had been many months since he had felt so out of focus. Looking at the key lock with its numbers back lit by a LED light with a gold glow, Dante's thoughts returned to the reason he was on this floor. "Pull yourself together, Dante. These next few minutes may be the most crucial ones in your life."

He was focused and ready by the time he stepped up to the senior secretary's desk. "Checking out the priorities of office before your meeting?" she asked, a grin on her face.

Susan was the manager of the slow pitch team, so he knew her well. She had a good sense of humor.

"Actually, I got turned around there, Susan. Not used to the carpeted floors and expensive wall coverings."

"That, too, shall pass," Susan said with a knowing smile, "they're waiting for you in the board room. The door on your left, just past my file cabinet."

Dante nodded and walked past her in the direction she was pointing. "Good luck," she said as he passed.

"Thanks," Dante replied, adding under his breath, "You have no idea how much I'm going to need it."

Walking through the doorway into the board room, and gazing at the faces looking up at him, Dante felt a feeling of confidence and control. The director whose son Dante had rescued rose from his chair and pointed to an empty seat across the table. After introductions, along with some brief small talk, they "got down to brass tacks," according to the senior vice president.

The scenario regarding the proposed position in Vancouver set out, the vice president asked the critical question. "Are you ready for the big move, Dante?"

"I've decided to pass on your very generous offer. I am just not ready to move so far away. You felt I was worthy of the position, and I am honored by that, but I'm sorry, I must turn it down. It is a wonderful opportunity, but it just isn't one I feel I can take at this time."

There was a long pause as the members of the board stared at him. Their mutual expression was dumbstruck. The father of the rescued canoeist was the first to speak, "do you realize what you are saying? Are you sure? This is an offer of a lifetime. Do you need a few moments to think about your answer?"

"No," said Dante, "As I said, I appreciate your offer, but I just can't accept it. I am so sorry."

"Very well," said the Vice President, "If that's your decision, then thank you for coming. I hope you realize offers like these are rare. It is unlikely there will be another opening soon. If your decision satisfies you, then it is my hope you will not regret it. You may leave."

"Thank you, sir," said Dante, rising from the chair and leaving the board room.

He made a few dance steps as he passed Susan's desk. "How did it go?" She asked.

"Fabulously!" Replied Dante and gave her a brief wave as he stepped through the open door of the elevator.

Susan would tell him later she had never seen the senior officers so upset. They didn't know how to react to Dante's refusal to accept the assistant directorship.

All Dante could think of as he took the elevator to his office floor was that Merilee would be there, and he was going to take her out for lunch.

Chapter 24. Golden Moments

Dinner with Merilee was a delight. Merilee suggested a nearby pub style restaurant one of her friends had recommended. "They have great taco's there, "she said with a grin, "you like Mexican, don't you?"

"I like tacos. I'm not sure how Mexican they are since they seem to be a popular item in

restaurants with black beer and Irish names."

They both laughed as they made their way to a table. They were able to find an alcove with a small table and two plush chairs set nearly side by side. Dante asked Merilee if she would like to share a bottle of wine with dinner. "Are you kidding," she responded with a coquettish smile, "tacos and wine. That's almost an oxymoron. I'd prefer a good-sized tankard of cold beer, thank you, and not the black stuff, please."

"Your wish is my command," returned Dante showing a playful grin

The server approached to take their order. "Two tankards of house ale and the biggest Taco plate you have and load it up with everything "

Within moments of ordering, they were tapping beer mugs together followed by a lubricating swig of the cool clear amber fluid and the tone of the evening was set.

When the Tacos arrived, the two of them roared with laughter. Dante had asked for the biggest taco plate the restaurant offered and they were more than accommodated. It was humongous! Conversation stopped as they dug in, fighting each other for the cheesiest chips. To be fair, Merilee was more interested in the guacamole and sour cream. Dante went for the cheese.

It may have been an enormous plate of tacos, but Dante had the appetite. Merilee did her share, consuming about a quarter of what was there. Dante ate the rest. Finished, they sat back and lifted their drinks in a second toast.

They polished off a second tankard of beer throughout an evening mixed with laughter and revelation. Dante told Merilee of his early life in a hippie commune while she confessed her less than exciting life growing up in the suburbs with an older sister, a younger brother, a father who loved monster trucks and a mother who calmly looked after them all.

Although astonished, she could only laugh to hear Dante's stories of the dangers of physical activity according to his parents. She showed him the scar on her knee she got when she fell while sprinting in a high school track meet. She told him how she shrugged off cheerleading, her sister's specialty in favor of athletics. Dante told her how he had to sneak into the gym to watch the volleyball team practice. She told him how she had captained her volleyball team to a second-place finish in a state tournament. She jumped up and gave an animated description of the game point. Jumping back from the chair, she called out, "mine," and crouched, extending her arms, and swinging upward.

She grinned at Dante as she intoned, "reception," then twisted sideways, throwing her arms up above her head and flicked her wrists. She leaned towards Dante, "That was set, "then she leaped up in the air and swung her hand from behind her ear, then turned to Dante again, "that was spike and point," and she added as she sat down, suddenly aware of others in the restaurant looking at her, "and that is one beer too many."

She roared with laughter again. Dante couldn't resist and joined in and for a few brief moments the restaurant was filled with laughter. "Guess I know how to play volleyball, now," he said.

'Bit more than that,' was Merilee's response, and they both laughed some more

Then Dante stopped, the room returned to normal. There was some distant laughter and sounds of conversation. "Well," grinned Merilee, "that's how we ended up with silver at the state championship; Regal Davis, a private school won the championship."

"Too bad," said Dante.

"Nah, they always won. I think that was their third of fourth in a row," Merilee shook her head, "And now, I think it's time to go home."

At that moment Dante fell in love.

The evening had been wonderful for both, but now it had come to an end. Because of what happened the last time, they both decided that it would be best to go their separate ways. Perhaps next time, but they both agreed it was a great evening and well worth repeating. They kissed goodbye at the door of Merilee's uber. The kiss lingered and Merilee hugged Dante who wasn't quite sure what he should be doing, so he lightly patted her back. Moments later, she was off, and Dante nearly danced all the way home.

Back at his apartment, Dante could barely contain his joy. The evening had been perfect, more than he could ever have expected. He was so happy he found himself humming the last song he had heard as he left the restaurant with Merilee. He flopped down on the bed, still humming and that's how he appeared on the pallet in purgatory, humming. Still humming, he jumped to his feet ready for action. He felt good and it showed. Astrada couldn't help but be impressed by his verve in all his practice engagements. Before long most of his opponents were icing bruises and bandaging elbows and wrists.

When Tauren showed up to find to how things went for Dante at the office that day, combat practice was finished, and Dante was working out on his own. Astrada couldn't restrain her tongue and blurted out that whatever was motivating Dante, he sure looked like a champion, besting all the sparring partners one after another. Tauren was surprised to hear Astrada speaking so positively about her charge. This was a first, and Tauren recognized a major breakthrough had occurred. This was good news. He approached Dante to see if there was any more interesting news, and there was.

Dante was able to explain how he had turned down the job. His cheerful demeanor and a smear of what Tauren immediately knew to be lipstick on his cheek told him much more. Dante was energized in a way he had never been before. While Tauren was well aware Dante's forming a relationship back on earth was problematic and could lead to trouble when battle was imminent, it could also inspire the champion in a more personal, less pedantic way. He had discouraged Dante from taking the promotion; he would remain silent on this and just observe.

Astrada was feeling generous towards her champion after watching him dispatch one after the other of his practice opponents with incredible ease. She sent him home early. He was surprised to learn that he didn't want to go. He expressed that to Astrada who replied, "all the available sparring partners are busy treating the aches and bruises you've already given them. Do you think they would be ready to get beaten up again so soon? Go home. Give them a day to heal."

Chapter 25. What's Wrong

The memory of his workout in purgatory might no longer be present in Dante's mind, but the exhilaration of the previous evening remained. He felt more rested than he had in weeks, and the combination of this and the memory of the dinner with Merilee put a bounce in his step as he made his way to work. He arrived at his desk twenty minute before the workday began and had just sat down when the director who had advocated for him with the executive showed up to face him. "Damn, Dante, what was that all about yesterday? If there was something bothering you about the promotion, why didn't you come to see me?"

"Sorry, sir," almost immediately, Dante's good feelings took a nosedive, "I had been wrestling with the decision, but really didn't know until they officially made the offer what my official answer would be."

"Well, you made me look like an idiot up there. I may never live it down. I had such confidence in you."

"And I appreciated it sir, I'm just not prepared to make that move right now."

"Why would that be, Dante? Something about the company bother you, or was it just the move?"

"It just didn't seem to be the right thing to do now. I'm not sure why I am so certain of that, but I am. I'm truly sorry if my decision has made it difficult for you."

"They'll get over it, but I can't see them offering you any promotion in the future. I'm not saying you're blackballed or anything, but they cut a lot of traditional corners in offering that position to you. It won't happen again."

"That's ok by me, sir. I am happy enough with what I'm doing and where I'm doing it."

What Dante couldn't tell him because he didn't understand it himself, was a sense of anticipation he had that something big was about to happen. "Well, Dante," said the director as he turned away from Dante's desk, "I'm still deep in your debt. You need anything, you know where to find me."

He didn't wait for a response but headed down the aisle between the cubicles towards the elevators, leaving Dante momentarily alone. It wasn't for long as Adam came through the door and sped directly to Dante's desk. Sitting on the edge of the desk, he swung around to face Dante and winked. "So, how'd it go, yesterday?"

"I told them I wasn't going to accept the promotion. They said it was fine, and I left."

"You know that's not what I'm talking about, Romeo," grinned Adam, "How was the date with Merilee?"

"Oh that," Dante looked down and casually shuffled the papers on the desk, "It went alright."

"Yeah, but what happened?" Adam was insistent.

"We talked, had tacos and a couple of beers."

"You took her home..."

"Sorry Adam," he said, as he pulled some papers from his inbox and began thumbing through them, "I have to do some work. I'm meeting with my department right after nine."

Adam didn't get to his supervisory position in the company without being able to recognize the brush off. Earl may have continued to press Dante, but not Adam. He knew the conversation was closed, for the time being. He jumped to his feet and slapped the top of the desk, "Have a good morning, pal. See you at lunch," and he left.

Dante's abrupt dismissal of him didn't bother Adam. His friend was shy. He knew he'd get the full scoop before the day ended.

Earl came by shortly after but was completely oblivious to everything. All he cared about was, were they going to have a drink after work. "You can ask Merilee along. She's fun and there are a couple of girls in my department could join us, so she won't feel outnumbered."

"Could do." Was all Dante said, but it was enough for Earl, and he left.

"See you at lunch," he called over his shoulder as he ran for the opening door of an elevator.

They had a couple of beers after work and Merilee and the two girls from Earl's department came along. It was pleasant, but everyone seemed distracted for one reason or another and the evening ended early. Each one went their own way. Adam got as much information as he was going to get when Merilee gave Dante a lingering kiss before heading off.

Things were quiet at the office for the next few weeks. There were some evenings and a seasonal social, but there was no clear news on the state of Dante and Merilee's relationship. That was the way they both liked it. Dante was still shy of bringing her to his apartment, only to somehow anger her as he had the first time. Of course, when he landed in purgatory, it clarified the concern until morning came again. Still, the effect of the dawning relationship between Dante and Merilee was making its mark in purgatory.

Dante was no longer just the champion in name only, he was in every way the champion. Every drill, every simulation, every activity he approached with gusto. He could outfight, outrun, out swim and even out ride all the warriors and sparing partners he came up against. When he bested Astrada in most things and was even a match for her with sword and dagger, it convinced her he had arrived. He exuded confidence, giving a running commentary of his sparing matches that sometimes ended with the sparring partner collapsing in pain and other times, collapsing in laughter.

His tactical skills matched his physical abilities. After Earl put some of Dante's limited video game activities on the internet, he received challenges from all around the world. Amateurs and professionals fell to his subtle play, their frustration growing at their lack of success against him and the limited times he went online to play. Many found his combination of tactical skill and reluctance to play often to be mysterious.

A mythology grew around him, constructed by gamers who felt he was a professional in disguise, or a developer, or some kind of genius. This bothered Dante and just as he concealed his rock-hard body in loose-fitting clothes, he stopped playing video games on the internet all together.

He played a few times offline with friends from the office; Earl and Adam and several others, but even if he handicapped himself, he still would end up winning. So, he stopped doing that all together and spent only a few minutes here and there on games, experimenting with different tactics, aiming for simplicity.

In purgatory Dante was, to use an old saw, at the top of his game. He was ready to meet Fluglaz's invading legions. Dante's fellow warriors were ready, too. Compared to Fluglaz's legions, they were few in number and this concerned Tauren who realized that it was time to go back to earth and start recruiting. It was around this time that the wise ones informed him that Fluglaz in the name of the Grand Duchy had put a large bounty on Astrada's head.

Not for the first in the near infinite life of purgatory, bounty hunters set out from many domains to earn the offered treasure and undying good will of the empire builder, Fluglaz. The bounty hunters represented a wide variety of species. Some looked nearly human, others sported the evolutionary summit of different ancestral origins; mammalian, insectile, reptilian, even piscine.

Fortunately for Astrada, they had no idea where to find her, so only a few were travelling toward earth's purgatory. There was no shortage of avarice or brutality among them. They didn't come as a group. The concept of sharing had no place in their focused minds. There were four of them coming, three by different routes and unknown to each other.

Slightly closer to the boundary of earth's purgatory were two brothers from a set of worlds where asexual reproduction vied with a more traditional sexuality. The two were a transmission of asexual reproduction, and were more like clones of each other than brothers, Arnog and Ranog. They worked together. What's more, they didn't look alien to the human eye. Except for the head ridge nearly covered with thick blue hair that also concealed small, fanlike ears, they could be easily taken for a fellow human except for the blue hair and slightly blue tinge to their skin.

Of all the bounty hunters en route, the blue twins were the least concerned about financial reward. They shared everything and were prepared to pay off anyone who would assist them, because what they really looked forward to was the dead or alive statement in the bounty contract by gleefully putting their victim somewhere between the two. The real payoff for them, it seems, was the pain and suffering they inflicted.

The large golden shaded eyes, long snout and vestigial tail while reflecting the reptilian origins of Ozolio, the second bounty hunter, could not conceal the look of intelligence in those enormous eyes. His form fitting combat wear was impeccable, stylish, and fit perfectly, its subtle hues enabling him to slip in and out of sight at will. If the statement in the bounty said dead or alive, he would return them dead, not because he was cruel, but because he was practical.

The domains of purgatory bounded by forbidding swamps and rocky desert regions made travelling any distance a grueling experience. Hard enough with the dead weight of a slowly decaying body thrown over the back of one's steed, but not nearly as messy as escorting an unhappy prisoner who was stubborn, resistant, had to be kept tied up and constantly needing to be watched even when relieving himself. He, presumably he was a he, was too fastidious for that.

The living could be so smelly and unpleasant, a little perfume, and the dead ceased to be much of an inconvenience. That much he could handle for the benefits he would receive, the reward that allowed him to continue living the comfortable lifestyle he preferred.

The last bounty hunter was a thing directly out of a nightmare. The faceted eyes and huge mandibles of its insectile ancestry seemed to clash with very uninsectlike nostrils and the vestigial pincers that framed its face. Its four thin multi-jointed arms ending in cruel looking caliper like talons were a fine contrast to the solid leather boots it wore on the similar appendages that served as its legs.

Its narrow thorax was longer, and its abdomen carried perpendicular to the ground was small. Matching the boots, it was dressed in a leather kilt. Bandoliers hung across its narrow shoulders, each holding a sword and ten darts for the small crossbow on the belt at its waist. The two antennae topping its head were festooned with gaily colored bands that accentuated the three shiny silver rings on each. While the other bounty hunters were similar in size to the people of earth's purgatory, it was several heads taller.

Oddly enough, this being was the least destructive. They classed it as a female in its domain, an ancient remnant of an even more ancient world. Its domain was poor, its associated worlds were ashen rocks in a rapidly shrinking universe. It had a large family it was responsible for, and bounty hunting put food on the eating boards. It was not cruel in the way the others were. It didn't relish killing, doing so only when left with no other choice. It was still brutal in that it showed no mercy, forcibly dragging the struggling bodies of its captives across the inhospitable terrain between the domains until bringing it to whoever offered the bounty; there to collect the reward and then return to care for its family until someone announced the next bounty. Its name? Unprintable in any human language and any attempt to utter it aloud would probably hurt.

None bode well for Astrada. Her one personal advantage, they did not know of her fighting skill. Nor did they know she was under the protection of the guardian of earth's purgatory and his champion. At the moment, the champion didn't know that either. He would learn soon.

Chapter 26. Stick Around

It was one thing to know there were those coming intending to collect a reward for Astrada and would be quite happy to bring her in dead. It was absolutely another thing not to know who these bounty hunters were or when they would appear. If this troubled if Astrada, it didn't show itself on the training field. In this, she was pragmatic. She was expecting this could happen and her life forfeit from the moment she faced Duke Davlos on the practice grounds intending to kill him. She was not deterred by it then and was not deterred by it now.

In the company of her trainees, as well as Dante, who had most certainly become the definitive champion, and the staunch and upright Tauren, she felt she was as ready as she could be to face down any bounty hunter. Knowing how many she might face would help, but no matter, she would deal with it whether it was three or thirty.

Needing little sleep and Tauren not needing any, she didn't stray far from him and her fellow warriors. She would be ready whenever the bounty hunters arrived. One thing she knew, she must be prepared for attacks to be simultaneous and from anywhere. Despite that, she knew well that these bounty hunters would be working on their own. Sharing was not a part of your average bounty hunters' credo.

Dante would arrive every earthly evening to work out. Hearing of the bounty placed on Astrada's head by Fluglaz, he was concerned for her. As champion, he was also a protector, and he felt a deep need to protect her. Not only was she his teacher, but she was a friend, one with whom he would happily join in battle. He decided to take some time off work and stay in purgatory as the threat seemed to be imminent. Tauren had tried to dissuade him. The call to meet the invaders would come soon enough, and for that it was likely Dante would have to sever all ties with his career back on earth. The recruiting process and the invasion force would do that. Dante insisted so Tauren would abide by that and use the time to prepare Dante to go back to earth fully aware of who and what he was.

Dante went back for one day to tell them at the office he had to spend some time with a sick relative that would take him out of town for a while. He hadn't taken a holiday in several years, so there was no problem getting the time off. He wanted to get out of the office before Adam, Earl or especially, Merilee found out. He left them notes, promising that he would be in touch. He was gone, nearly running down the street to be out of sight from anyone who might be curious about who he was visiting and where.

The real problem was, he didn't know the answer himself. He wasn't really sure why he had asked for the time off and why it had seemed so imperative that he do so. He felt he needed to go home and pack a bag for some undetermined trip. When he got to his apartment, he felt compelled to lie down on his bed and rest, but for the moment he resisted going to the hall closet. He got his overnight bag from the kitchen closet, then returned to his room to gather some clothes. His bag packed, he gave in to the call of his bed and lay down. Instantly it was all clear to him.

Since he was going to be around, Astrada and Tauren drafted him to train some new recruits Tauren had gathered from the furthest reaches of earth's purgatory and from surrounding domains. He took on the role with gusto. Following in the footsteps of his teacher, he put the recruits through their paces with the same level of intensity. They would be exhausted, sore, and better fighters within a few days. He and Astrada were busy with their charges on the practice field when news came in that a pair of blue tinted twins were asking about Astrada. On hearing this, Tauren joined the trainees in the Stade.

They were planning to take a few of the more skilled warriors and intercept the two and escort them from the domain. To their surprise, as they were preparing to head off, the two brothers appeared at the Stade Arcanium. It became clear that the honest and protective posture of Astrada's associates was beyond the twins' understanding. All their experience up until then was of greed, cruelty, and double dealing.

Based on this, they offered a large share of their bounty to Tauren, Dante and their warriors if they would turn Astrada over to them. One brother held up a roll of papyrus with one hand and pointed at it with the other, "This Astrada is a murderer, slayer of The Duchess and other members of the court. This document with the sigil of Duke Fluglaz will inform you he hopes to avenge the Duchess Clarvita's death and punish the evildoer. The document also states we are here as his agents. He has called for the slave, Astrada's return, dead or alive. On his authority, we demand you hand her over. You will be well rewarded."

"THERE WILL BE NO TURNING over of anyone to the likes of you," shouted Dante, brandishing his sword. "Astrada is our companion in arms and is here under the protection of the guardian, myself, and all the warriors you see. I suggest you return to your Duke Fluglaz and tell him his agents are not welcome here, nor is he."

"Tough talk," intoned Tauren in a quiet aside to the angry champion.

At Dante's words, the two brothers, seeing they were outnumbered, quickly turned, and left the Stade. They disappeared through a large crowd of atoners who had gathered outside,

"You know they will not give up," said a grim Astrada, "they won't be too far away just watching for their chance to get me alone."

"Then we will not let you be alone," Dante's tone was adamant.

Tauren and Astrada were both impressed. They recognized the command and absolute conviction in his voice. Singling out three of the more experienced warriors, Dante instructed them to keep a close watch on the two brothers. He and some others would stay with Astrada.

Both Tauren and Astrada recognized the type. They knew the two brothers were ruthless, sadistic creatures who would stop at nothing to get their hands on Astrada. They would be a threat as long as they were alive. Dante was still a neophyte with the reality of the many beings to be found within the realms of purgatory. He hoped that they would quickly understand their prey was well protected by highly skilled fighters and leave. Sadly, Dante had no idea.

Chapter 27. Death is Death

After the encounter with the blue brothers, Arnog and Ranog, Astrada could not sleep, or even rest. She couldn't keep this up forever and eventually had to leave the Stade and go to her room for a rest. Dante sent Astrada to her apartment with an escort of four warriors. He would be along a few minutes later after he finished drilling his recruits. Dante's trackers were monitoring the twin bounty hunters, and he was continuously receiving information about their movements. At any moment he expected an update, and then he would make his way to Astrada's home and join the other guards.

The expected information did not come, so he made his way to Astrada's place. As he neared her home, he could see a dark heap in a shady corner between two buildings. This was unusual. It hadn't been there the last time he passed. He had to look.

Earlier, a pair of the warriors Dante had sent to follow the twins saw they were making their way toward Astrada's place. One was to return to Dante to tell him where the two were going. The other would continue to follow. As he followed, the twins turned a corner and briefly disappeared from his sight. He raced up to the corner to improve his vantage point, only to step right into the blade of Arnog's double-edged sword. As he stumbled backward, the bounty hunter withdrew the sword from the wound and slashed him across the face. The warrior fell to the ground, writhing in his death throes.

The other warrior had not gotten far when he was grabbed from behind and a razor-sharp dagger slashed his throat, severing the jugular. It was Ranog, dagger in hand, he held on to the dying warrior long enough to drag him to a picket fence and forcibly impale him on it.

The heap Dante had seen was the first warrior, lying in a pool of blood. This warrior and his companion would, each on his own, be reanimating, in some unknown area of earth's purgatory, to the need for atonement with only sketchy memories of what had happened to them.

On recognizing the dead warrior, Dante wasted no time with the body that would soon be dust, but raced toward Astrada's home, sword drawn. Reaching the front door, he nearly tripped over the body of one of her guards. Another was on the stairs to her rooms. The dying warrior on the stairway wheezed the words, "not them," as Dante sprinted by. The door to Astrada's room had been flung wide, but the window shades were all drawn, making it hard to see.

Dante darted through the living room towards Astrada's sleeping quarters, calling out her name as he went. Inside the room, there was little light to let him see. He stepped to the nearest window and with his free hand pulled the shades from it. Whirling to face the bed, he saw someone was there, but it wasn't Astrada. It was one twin, lying on the pallet as a pool of blue blood, as pale as the blue of his skin soaked into the covers. There was no sign of Astrada.

From behind him, an agonized voice shouted, "You killed him! Die!"

Dante spun towards it, sword at the ready. Simultaneously, he reached with his free hand for the dagger at his waist. It was the second twin, eyes wide, sword ready to drive into Dante's chest. Astrada had trained Dante well. Even before he was fully facing the enraged Ranog, he parried his thrust, stepped past the outstretched blade, and swept his sword in a horizontal slash. The battle honed blade separated the bounty hunter's head cleanly. He had only a beat to register his surprise before his head toppled from his body and he collapsed to the floor. It happened so fast; Dante didn't have time to register what he had done. He leapt past the crumbling Ranog to the stairs.

The dying warrior on the stairs reached out as Dante was passing. Dante stopped to look down at him. The warrior grabbed Dante's ankle, "Those eyes," he groaned, "Those eyes, so big, so fast," he coughed, and his hand slipped free of Dante, and his eyes were suddenly flat and staring. Another loss to Tauren's expeditionary force. He might come back as an atoner but could only defend within the boundaries of earth's purgatorial domain.

In the forest, just beyond the boundary of the enormous urban area of that part of earth's purgatory, Ozolio had made camp, and he was angry. He hadn't expected to meet the blue twins. He was forced to fight one of them; he didn't know which, but during the fight, the twin had slashed Ozolio's favorite leather jacket through to the skin. The wound the twin's blade inflicted on him wasn't deep but needed to be patched. He was more upset about the jacket. It was cut beyond repair and the lining destroyed by the blood from his wound. He was angry, too, that despite everything he had done to subdue her, Astrada was a vicious fighter and it had taken him way longer than he wanted to get her under control and tied up. The hasty get away was the only reason the girl was still alive.

Ozolio decided he would dispatch her after he took care of the business of cleaning up. While Ozolio was closing his wound with a heated knife, putting on a bandage, and rinsing his jacket in the small nearby stream, hoping to make it passable for the journey back to Fluglaz, Astrada was busy, too. One trick she had learned was to fasten a small bit of metal to her first and middle fingernails. Invisible under the paint she had put on all her nails, a tiny razor-sharp edge projected ever so slightly past the end of her actual nail. While her captor was fussing over his jacket, Astrada was using the sharp edges attached to her nail to cut and free herself from her bonds.

The lizard man came over and sat beside her. She had freed her hands but was still feigning unconsciousness. "Well, little missy, I expect you hear me. I am about to prepare for a very long and arduous journey back to Grand Duke Fluglaz. You will be less of a burden if I dispatch you now. So, if you'll just continue to hold still, I will make it quick."

Squinting, she could see the dagger in his hand reaching out to her. She was about to roll away from the blade when she saw her capture suddenly start and then to look away from her. He jerked again, and the dagger flew from his hand and landed where she could easily grab it. She opened her eyes to see what had happened. Two small darts protruded from his body. One had penetrated his side, the other was near his temple. There was a dazed expression on his face, his huge eyes staring off in the direction the darts had come from. A third dart caught him in the face, and he rolled forward.

Astrada, who was familiar with many different looking creatures from her travels though purgatory and the science world, was now looking at the most horrific being she had ever seen. The unnameable insectile bounty hunter was reloading her dart gun when Astrada leapt to her feet, dagger in hand and. The creature stopped working on the gun and reached with one of her four hands for a sword on her bandolier. Astrada flung her dagger and dove for the crumpled body of Ozolio and his sword. As the hunter grasped its sword, pulling it free from the bandolier, the spinning dagger caught its arm just above the caliper-like talons severing it. The creature's sword fell to the ground. With another of its hands, it reached for its second sword. Astrada was on it.

The bounty hunter was tough, but thanks to Davlos and her training program with Dante, Astrada was a finely tuned killing machine. She knew right away that the bizarre anatomy of the creature might limit her killing strokes. Instantly she decided that without eyes, her assailant would be at a real disadvantage, and so she went for the head. The bounty hunter was slow. It did most of its battling with the dart gun. Its sword work was rough and aggressive, and the extra hands with their deadly looking talons were another inconvenience. Slashing, Astrada severed another arm. She then leaped to the hunter's side, avoiding a sweeping blow that would have cut her in half had it landed. She paid no mind to what might have been and focused on the head area of the creature. Jumping as high as she could, holding the sword in both her hands, she swung it with all her might. There was a crunching sound as it bit into the carapace. The insectile bounty hunter's head lolled to one side, held on by a single piece of ligament.

The headless hunter continued to slash with its blade, but Astrada had moved out of reach. She watched as the creature continued to flail around, unseeing. After some time, it slowed and sat down hard on the ground. Its thoughts in that moment were on who would be the next provider for the family back home. It wouldn't be her.

As Astrada checked the lizard man's body to make sure he was dead and to relieve him of any other weapons, he might have on him, the insectile bounty hunter rose from the ground and walked back the way it had come. Astrada would never know nor care that it eventually ended up sucked into quicksand in the swamp that separated earth's domain from its neighbors. It would eventually find its family, but as a domain locked atonement seeker, not as a provider.

Chapter 28. What Have I Done?

Astrada had just marked the site where the lizard man bounty hunter's remains could be found and was making her way towards the city when she met Tauren and Dante on their way to find her. Dante's relief on seeing her uninjured was palpable. He leapt from his horse, ran to her, and pulled her into a full bear hug. To be sure, Astrada was a little taken aback by Dante's reaction, but she immediately recognized that it was good to have friends.

Back at the Stade Arcanium, the bodies of the dead were assembled on the training field floor. The bodies, even those of the enemy, would be honored with a brief ceremony before they decayed and fell to dust. The breakdown of the corpses of the living was rapid and complete in purgatory. Within a day or two they would be gone, leaving only a small pile of grey ash behind. Here, Dante saw the consequences of his sword play for the first time. The body of the blue twin he had fought, if such a brief encounter could even be technically termed a fight, was stretched out with his head beside him. He had killed someone. That someone may have been a species other than human, but to Dante's eyes, he was human. He was, fully sentient and Dante had ended his life with the slice of a sword.

Dante was despondent. This was way outside his experience. The training, an ordeal at first, became more enjoyable as his skills improved, but on the training field there might be cuts and bruises, but no-one died. The others tried to raise his spirits by reminding him that the man he killed would by now be reanimated somewhere in his own domain of purgatory. The remains were no longer his. "Then why are we honoring him?" wondered Dante.

"We honor all the living who have died," explained Tauren, "some we might see again, but they will never be quite the same as they have passed over to a different stage of existence."

This did little to boost Dante's spirits as he recalled in great detail his swing of the sword cleaving head from body, the brief look of surprise in the blue twin's eyes and the head sliding free of the body to fall to the floor. This and the fact that he had sent six warriors to their deaths troubled him deeply.

Tauren had told Dante that the next time he returned to earth, he would have complete recall of his time in purgatory and would be actively if inconspicuously seeking potential recruits to the cause. On seeing Dante's reaction to his first kill, Tauren decided it was not the time for Dante to retain full knowledge when he returned to earth. Since the wise ones had informed him that no more bounty hunters were proceeding their way, Tauren sent Dante back as he always had, with no memory of his time in purgatory.

It was midday when Dante woke up in his bedroom back on earth. He felt totally washed out and a little sad and didn't understand why. He needed to be active, so he decided to go back to work. On his arrival, friends and staff greeted him warmly, asking about his sick friend and the trip. For a moment Dante was non-plussed, then remembered that he had taken several days off and the story he had given as the excuse. He quickly concocted a tale to support his earlier story. He finished by telling them everything was fine, so he came home.

The name of the mid-west city he gave was for a place small enough to be obscure to most so no one could easily trace his steps and find out he hadn't gone there or known anyone who lived there.

While most of his fellow workers accepted the details of his fabricated story without question, Merilee and his closest friends saw something different. To them, Dante was clearly upset and depressed. Their explanation to themselves was that whoever Dante went to see, things hadn't worked out well. Perhaps the ailment, whatever it was, was not improving. They offered to take him out after work, and he agreed.

The evening was pleasant. Adam, Earl, and even Merilee did most of the talking. Dante responded with appropriate laughter, but they saw he was still distracted. "What's wrong, Dante?" asked Merilee.

Although at the moment he didn't know why, he blurted out, "How would you feel if you killed someone?"

Adam and Earl went silent as Merilee asked, "Dante, you didn't kill anyone, did you?"

"No, but somehow I feel like I did. It's really strange, and it bothers me. What really bothers me though is that it didn't seem to trouble me very much, like it was the right thing to do. It feels almost real."

"Dante, did something happen to you in Wichita, a car accident, or something."

"Wichita," thought Dante, "why did he tell them he had gone to Wichita?"

It was a place he had heard of in a cowboy movie or something similar when he was young, and he liked the name. He had told them he was going to look after a sick cousin in

Wichita, but he knew he had never been to Wichita. In fact, now that he really thought about it, he realized he had been away from work for nearly a week and had no memory of what he had done in all that time. Maybe he went to Wichita. Maybe he had a car accident, and he or someone he was with had killed someone. It was possible trauma had made him forget. The forgetting troubled him, but interestingly the other thought didn't. Whatever had happened, he was not unhappy about it. It was just the one vague thing concerning him, and it had something to do with killing and necessity. He wondered if soldiers felt this way. At least they knew why.

This all flashed through his mind in a split second. "Nothing happened in Wichita," was all he could say. "It's a lovely place, and the weather was nice. The Magnolias were in blossom around the courthouse."

He didn't know if any of it was true. He hadn't checked the weather report there for the last week. He assumed there would be a courthouse but knew absolutely nothing about Magnolias. He doubted Adam and Earl did either, and he was hoping Marilee wasn't an expert on Magnolias, because they might not even grow there. Luckily, it turned out she wasn't.

Over the next few days Dante's bad feelings began to fade.

Chapter 29. Accept and Recruit

His earth leave over, Dante returned to purgatory and immediately recalled what had been troubling him. Although the thought he had killed someone disturbed him, when he saw Astrada, fierce and ready for action, he felt much better. He had had no choice; it was kill or be killed and the killing was motivated by his desire to assist Astrada, his guide and instructor. He couldn't justify killing, but he could justify the cost of providing protection.

As champion of a purgatorial domain, Dante was obliged never to enjoy or even accept killing another sentient being. As war chief, the main role of the champion and protector, his warrior training was an essential component of the position. It meant he would find himself in situations where he might have to kill or order his forces into battle, where they might kill or, tragically, be killed. As the philosopher said, the mantle of responsibility does not rest lightly, or something to that effect. This was what Dante needed to come to terms with before the advance marauders of Fluglaz's army made it to earth's domain.

His training and his work with the recruits became more intense. Some of the enjoyment that had developed as his skills improved faded. It wasn't the anguish that he felt in those early times, but he no longer looked upon it as an advanced Physical Education class in high school. It was exactly what Astrada had been trying to impress on him. This was serious business.

Fluglaz was intent on conquest, and any dominion under his subjugation would not only lose its independence but also its wealth, as he would demand tribute after tribute until there was no more to give. The inhabitants, both the living and the atoners, would be subject to terrible oppression at the hands of the cruel and ruthless henchmen Fluglaz would leave in charge. Dante was the champion, and it was his duty to do whatever was necessary to prevent that.

This was the champion's final lesson, and he passed with the proverbial flying colors. Tauren was now confident Dante was ready to face the major game changer of knowing who and what he was all the time. He will carry that knowledge back to earth's plane and immediately discover everything had changed. His work will be meaningless to him, and he won't be able to give it more than cursory attention. With that will come the recognition he has no need for the job. His relationship with his friends may completely change. He'll learn being a champion is not a nine to five, or even an eleven to six position.

One of Dante's most difficult earthly responsibilities would be to recruit. Tauren had begun the process sometime earlier. In short order he learned modern living humans, while they had many odd beliefs, were collectively sceptics. Those expressing belief in purgatory would not consider it an actual place living beings could get to without dying. Many others had no belief at all in the concept. Others had a fairy tale view of another dimension and while Tauren knew that many other dimensions existed and in nearly infinite numbers, they weren't all that different from this one.

The only real magical realms were found in folktales and mythologies, the constructs of make believe and primitive fears. All this made it nearly impossible to convince anyone of purgatory's present reality. And, with Fluglaz's legions on the march, it was a real problem.

Tauren was honest with himself. Dante's work among his fellows would be close to impossible, but he would have to try, and hopefully not appear to be moon struck. What was their word for it, lunatic? Dante was, however, the champion and his powers of leadership and tactical skills might be of some help. It would remain to be seen, but time was running short. The need to gather what recruits they could and train them was becoming imperative.

Dante would require a few days to come to terms with his new reality, but he would have to be the champion and not take too long getting down to business. Tauren outlined all of this to Dante in a short meeting at which he gave him a silver ring with a small blue stone that would light up to show him where the portals to purgatory could be found. It would also help Tauren know which portal he was near so he could send escorts for anyone he sent through.

Other recruiters were busy combing the earth for volunteers, so Dante need not go too far from home to search out his. This would be a challenge, even for the champion, as people in this part of the world could be hard-headed. Tauren didn't expect them to be coming in by the thousands, but even a few would be helpful to the cause.

Finally, Tauren brought Dante to a nearby portal that would take him to a new portal in his room so he could come and go without the bed and pallet and wished him well. Dante stepped through and found himself in his bedroom closet. "Nice," he thought, as he opened the door to his room. He dressed for work and stepped out into the bright light of morning.

As he made his way to work, the knowledge of what he had been doing in purgatory while vivid seemed surreal and fantastical when contrasted with the familiar busy streets of his hometown. The office building with its large entrance and coffee shop in the foyer could not have been more different from his memories of the training grounds in purgatory. He could see the CEO standing with a large coffee in his hand, talking to other directors near the front doors. He nodded and greeted fellow workers as he stepped into the elevator to take him to his floor.

As usual, he was one of the first to arrive. He sat at his desk and shifted some papers around. Considering all he remembered, they didn't seem that important. Was purgatory the reality and this the dream? There was no question. He was fully aware they both were realities. It was just hard to put it all together in this mundane world of cubicles and computers. Things brightened immeasurably when Merilee came in. Just her waving as she went to hang up her jacket made him feel better.

That went all awry when she stepped up to his desk, a grin on her face, asking, "Ok, boss, what's on tap for today? Month's end's coming up."

The grin he loved, the words not so much. "Oh yeah," he answered, his voice expressionless, "No biggy! Let's keep it low key today, I've got a lot on my mind," and he wasn't wrong about that.

Chapter 30. New Me

Merilee couldn't remember Dante ever talking like this before. Usually, he focused on work when it was work time. This obvious disinterest was, for her, Dante being completely out of character. "What's wrong with you, Dante? Are you feeling alright? I thought you had gotten out of the dumps last week."

"I'm not in the dumps, Merilee, fact is I'm seeing things clearer than I ever have, and I now see this is only filler for me."

"Wow," Merilee was amazed. She would never have expected Dante to talk this way, "Let's talk about this, boss."

"Boss, shmoss, I'm just Dante, Merilee, and I'd love to talk about it... if it made any sense to me, at all."

Merilee's curiosity was peaked. She wasn't sure who this Dante was, but she knew she liked and cared for him as much as ever. "Ok, when do you want to talk?"

At first Dante wasn't sure if it was something he was ready to talk about, but then, this was Merilee. To his surprise, he discovered he did want to talk. He wanted to reveal his secret, as bizarre and disturbed as it might make him look. "Sure, let's go now. We can grab breakfast."

"Now! It's ten to nine," Merilee looked around perplexed, "We have work to do."

Dante laughed, "I looked at the schedule and like I said, it's no biggy. We can spare a couple of hours. I'm the boss in the section. No-one will miss us. Grab your jacket, let's go. Cafe

Bleu is a good spot. Hear they have a great all day breakfast menu."

Merilee was hesitant. Dante could see the uncertainty in her expression as she glanced out toward the room then back at him. "Really, don't worry. We're not a time clock. And, I really need to talk. If you're worried, I'll come up with an excuse. Maybe we need a white board or something, and you are my consultant."

With some reluctance, Merilee agreed. They were going through the foyer when Dante noticed Earl about to come into the building. He grabbed Merilee by the arm and dragged her to an alcove near the elevators. Earl walked by without noticing them, which was exactly what Dante wanted. Merilee raised her arm to wave at him when Dante put his face close to hers and said, "shhh!"

This was a far more forceful Dante than Marilee had seen before. Why was he trying to avoid Earl? "Come on," Dante gave her a big smile before turning toward the door.

That was new, too, and she had to admit, she really liked it.

As it turned to, Cafe Bleu had an excellent breakfast menu, and the coffee was first class. For the first few minutes Dante scanned the menu without saying a word, then sipped his coffee while Merilee looked on, a little confused. "Drink your coffee. Marilee, it's delicious."

"I thought you needed to talk, Dante,"

"Yes, you're right. I'm just not sure how to begin."

Marilee could now see Dante's discomfort. She had to admit he had hidden it very well. She tried to be helpful, "You know when I have something I want to talk about, I find the best thing is to just come out with it. I don't think you could tell me anything that would shock me."

Boy, was she wrong. Purgatory? Earth's champion? Invading warriors... in purgatory. Merilee was thinking she was seeing a far different side of Dante than the one she knew. This was the severely delusional Dante. Yet, as she listened, she had to admit that some of what he said had a ring of truth. His disappearing through the bed on her visit to his place made about as much sense as any of the other things about it she had speculated on. His amazing physical transition, his speed, awareness, catching a knife by the blade, his newly discovered athletic prowess. The rough water rescue and that story from Adam about him catching a crossbow bolt in mid-flight. These all caused her to wonder if there was some truth to what he was saying... but purgatory.

"I need to recruit for the coming invasion," said Dante, who was fully aware of how absolutely odd that sounded.

"The invasion in... purgatory?"

"Yes," Dante reached across the table to clasp her hand, "we need smart, strong, athletic people to join our ranks."

Dante paused, then looked at her with an eager expression on his face, "You would be perfect. Astrada is a superior personal combat trainer, she could turn you into a superb warrior. Want to see?"

Merilee was developing some concern for her boss and close friend, especially when, while waiting for her to respond, he calmly began to eat his order of bacon and eggs the waitress had set there earlier. Merilee could only pick at hers. She wasn't sure if she should be frightened or maintain a respectful mien.

"Seriously," he said, "come home with me after work and I will prove it to you."

Dante had made the offer, although he wasn't a hundred percent certain he could prove it at all. He had to admit to himself that it all sounded strange. There was always the chance, encouraged by a small nagging doubt, that he really was delusional, but it all just seemed too real. He realized he had made a bold and worrisome offer. He was not sure if she would accept. "Ok, Dante," Marilee said with a slightly harder than usual smile, I'll come with you after work, and we can visit purgatory together."

Neither was certain that she meant it, and well aware of how far out his story was, Dante was prepared to accept that she would refuse.

The rest of the day raced by. Back at work, Dante didn't seem much different from usual. He joined Adam and Earl in the lunchroom and discussed sports. They studiously avoided broaching the subject of his coming to work late or his coming in together with Merilee. Merilee, on the other hand, was far too agitated by Dante's story and his strange offer to be able to do much of anything. She stayed in the office, taking lunch at her desk. She nibbled at her sandwich, lost in deep thought. She kept coming back to the same questions. What was going on with Dante, and should she go home with him after work? A definitive answer to either of them was, for the moment, beyond her.

Merilee had to admit that some aspects of his story appealed to her. She knew she was not the cheerleader type. Thoughts of learning to fight and to serve as a warrior in this medieval style of war enthused her. If only it was real.

As the workday ground to a close, Merilee watched Dante with eagle eyes to see if there was any odd behavior. She saw none. He was helpful when an employee asked for help. He went around the department from time to time and was very solicitous of those busy working. As always, he was there to assist, but never imposed himself. She was feeling relaxed by quitting time, so when Dante walked up to her desk and asked, "Are you coming?" Merilee felt confident enough to decide she was.

Dante was important to her, and if he was delusional, she would rather be there to talk him through it than send him off on his own with who knows what consequences. Dante helped her on with her jacket and taking her by the arm, walked out the door and along the street towards his apartment. All Merilee could think as he engulfed her arm in his was, "So far, so good."

Chapter 31. What the Purgatory!

The walk to Dante's apartment, right up to his opening the front door, was an evaluation session for Marilee. She kept one eye on Dante most of the way, watching his expressions, listening to his tone, trying to figure out if he was dangerously crazy or totally delusional. She had to admit, in either case, he was doing an excellent job of hiding it. He was charming, funny, and as always, polite, and respectful. At his apartment, he unlocked the door and held it open for her to enter. Before crossing the threshold, she gave him a questioning glance, then stepped through.

She stiffened ever so slightly as he shut the door behind. "Right this way," he said, "indicating the door to his bedroom."

"Really, the bedroom?" Merilee couldn't stop herself.

"Sorry," Dante smiled diffidently, "I realize this may seem a little personal, and no doubt presumptuous considering our relationship up to now. However, it is a lot better than having to lie down on the bed since Tauren moved the portal into the closet."

"Yeah, for sure," Merilee laughed as she stepped into the room, "It is too early for that both figuratively and practically."

Dante wasn't exactly sure how to respond, so he pointed at the closet door. "It's right through there."

"The closet?" Merilee said with a tight laugh, "I think I read the book. Can we call this a wardrobe, and will there be a witch in the wardrobe?"

"Not exactly," laughed Dante, "and I realize just how silly this must seem. Oh, and you may think you will hit the back wall, but just keep walking,"

He took her hand and guided through the door. It was a bit of a tight fit. Dante couldn't remember being this intimate with anyone not wielding a knife. Merilee's eyes were wide open. Dante was right, it felt silly. There were better and less strange ways to get close. Hanging out in a closet wasn't her idea of intimacy, but he seemed so intense and serious about it she shrugged and went along. He shoved the few things on the hangers aside and stepped up to the back wall. "This is crazy," she thought, then she watched his foot and leg pass through the wall, and she thought, "This is crazy!"

There was no physical sensation as she moved through the wall, but there was a brief moment when she wanted to scream, turn, and run out of there just as fast as she could. Then she was through the portal. She and Dante were hand in hand on the edge of what looked like a large playing field for some unknown sport. She could barely believe her eyes as she gazed out at the large group of armored people who had turned, training swords and daggers in hand, to look at her. They all looked fierce even the females among them. There was one or two who barely looked human. The handsome giant, standing with them, walked over to her. He looked at Dante and smiled, "I see you've done some early recruiting," and turning to Merilee reached out his hand in an earthly greeting, "I'm Tauren. I'm sure you are feeling confused right now, but I want you to know you are welcome."

"Merilee," said a wide-eyed Merilee as she shook the gorgeous giant's hand.

His smile won her over immediately. She didn't know why, but the sight of him made her feel comfortable and safe. He turned and stretched out his hand towards the most beautiful woman she had ever seen. "This is Astrada, our training master, she will help Dante show you around."

Astrada introduced herself to Merilee, and Merilee made a shy response. Dante grinned. "Astrada is terrific, best swordsman, uh, woman in the domain, maybe in all of purgatory. If you decide to train with her, she will turn you into a super warrior in no time at all."

Astrada made no response and carefully hid a satisfied smile. The three set off to check out some of the local area. Although the odd variety of building, the well-groomed parkland, the cobbled streets were all fascinating as was Dante's running commentary, she saw Dante and Astrada seemed comfortable together and although she couldn't really put her finger on it, something about it bothered her. It didn't take long for her to realize what she was feeling was a smidgen of jealousy. How could she compete with this absolute knockout of a woman? She appeared to have everything, including a vicious-looking sabre and a razor-sharp dagger.

This feeling faded as Dante kept excitedly grabbing her hand and pointing out one landmark or another. While Dante was explaining everything he knew about purgatory, especially earth's domain, and pointing out the various period dress of the atoners, she was more distracted than the atoners seemed to be. "This is the strangest, most realistic dream I've ever had," kept running through her head.

Purgatory was a strange place with its shadowless light, its curious array of modern and archaic structures and its teaming population of atoners, all so quiet and introspective. Walking the streets around the Stade Arcanium seemed dreamlike. Still, Astrada, the big guy, and the training warriors seemed very real. "I hope I remember this when I wake up," she said in a quiet voice, "What a story to tell."

"Well, Merilee," Astrada turned to her as they came back into the Stade, "If you're interested, when you come back tomorrow, we can begin your training. You seem to be much fitter than Dante was when he first arrived."

Merilee had to admit to herself the prospect was intriguing. She would love the opportunity to learn some technics a warrior might use for defense. "Sure," she said enthusiastically, "I'd love to," quietly adding, "If only...."

"Time to go home," Dante took Merilee's arm and led her to a doorway in the nearest wall.

Moments later, the two were back in Dante's closet. They didn't stop until they were in the kitchen. "A coffee before I take you home," asked Dante, opening a cupboard and taking out a coffee tin.

Merilee demurred. All she wanted to do was get home, or whatever it might take to wake up in her own bed. Dante offered to walk her, but she said, "no," she'd call a cab. At home she sat on the edge of her bed for close to an hour before finally laying down and falling asleep. A few hours later, she woke up with no memory of the night before. As she prepared for work, the recollections slowly filtered back. They were indistinct and were only a half-remembered dream.

Within the framework of the vague remembrances, were brief glimpses of things that hinted of reality. Those brief memories were unsettling, otherwise it was a fascinating dream.

Chapter 32. It was Real?

The dream was captivating, and Merilee couldn't let it go. She just had to share it. Luckily it was Saturday, and every Saturday morning she met with several friends from her high school volleyball team. All fitness buffs, they hiked, biked, and worked out together when they could. When they couldn't, they got together for coffee at a local bistro and traded stories about their week. Other than a few stories about Dante, Merilee was a better listener than a raconteur. This time she had an intriguing tale to tell, even if it was only a dream.

Merilee couldn't remember everything, but she recalled the training field and the warriors, some practicing with different weapons, others doing strenuous workouts. Her friends were wide eyed as she told them about the handsome giant and fist pumped when she mentioned the knockout gorgeous woman training the lot of them. She was the one responsible for Dante buffing up. "Oh lord," said one of the girls, "That sounds fabulous. I'd love to train with a super-hot warrior queen."

The others around the table nodded in agreement and raised their coffee cups in a toast, "To super-hot warrior queens."

One closest to Merilee grabbed her sleeve, "Too bad it was a dream. It sounds so interesting and intense."

"Why can't I have great dreams like that," said another in a wistful voice.

"I know," smiled Merilee, "it seemed so real. Funny thing is still seeming to be real."

"Well," giggled the one who had grabbed her arm, "If it is real, I'm in."

"What sort of place was it, anyway?" asked one.

"In the dream, Dante said it was purgatory."

"I heard of it in school. I went to a catholic school. It's a place where you go when you die, to make up for your sins before going to heaven."

"Yes," nodded Merilee, "and they're there, but living people can go there and it's made up of many different domains, like, there are so many groups of beings, many not human, but all, I think the word the warrior queen used was, sentient."

"That's a pretty detailed dream you had, Merilee. It almost sounds like an actual place. Or are you plotting out a novel? Whatever it is, put me in it."

"Me too!"

"And me."

They all agreed this was the kind of place where they'd like to spend some time. If Merilee was writing a novel about this place, then they wanted to be included among the warriors. Little did they know it, but they were about to become some of Dante's first recruits for his army. Now they were enjoying each other's company and discussing a potential camping trip, and Merilee's dream slipped back into the background until her cell phone rang. It was Dante.

"Hi Merilee, I just called to see how you were doing after yesterday's visit to purgatory. What did you think?"

"Is that you, Dante?" Merilee asked.

"Yes, am I interrupting something. I'll let you go. I just wanted to ask you what you thought about yesterday and I'll let you go."

"Yesterday was great,"

"Ok, great, ready to go back?"

"Huuh?" Merilee was puzzled, "back?"

"Yeah, to purgatory. Hey, you sound distracted. I guess you're busy. I'll call you later. Bye."

"Dante, Dante, don't hang up," but it was too late, he was gone.

Merilee turned to her fellows at the table. "Did my phone just ring?"

"Yeah, it did, and you answered it," responded one of the women.

"Did you know who I was taking to?" Merilee asked this as if she wasn't quite sure what the answer would be.

"You said the name Dante, so I'm guessing that's who it was," said another of her friends.

Merilee clicked to her recent calls and held the screen of her phone up for the others to see, "So, according to this, who did I get my last call from?"

"Dante," they all chimed in in unison while one of them leaned over the table for a closer look and added, "And, less than a minute ago, so what's going on with you?"

"I don't know," said an anxious sounding Merilee, "but you have to come with me."

She got to her feet, pushed her cup back from the edge of the table, and stood up. The others stood up with her, their expressions as confused as hers, only for a different reason. "What's up? Where are we going?" asked one of them.

The others nodded their heads to show they agreed with the speaker. "To Dante's place," said Merilee.

"Hmm," said the one who had spoken earlier, "yeah, let's gang up on him. He won't stand a chance," she hesitated, then with a perplexed look added, "for whatever it is."

The former volleyballers picked up their gym bags and followed Merilee out to the street. "Let's take my car since it's parked closest to here."

Moments later they were in Marilee's car. As she pulled out onto the street one of her friends groaned. "I think we'd have been better in my car. It's an SUV."

"There you go, Carol, "laughed the one beside her, thinking of your own creature comforts. I think this is sort of cozy."

"Why are we all going to your almost boyfriend's place, anyway?" asked the one sitting in the passenger seat next to Merilee.

"So, you can tell me if he's crazy and if I'm crazy, too, and should find me a shrink."

"I love a good mystery," said one woman in the back seat, and moments later they were all chattering and occasionally offering a gentle tease Merilee's way.

Answering the door and finding Merilee and her four friends there surprised Dante, and he immediately began apologizing for the state of his apartment. "Seen worst," said one of the women.

"Yeah, Joan, I believe that was your place," laughed another.

"Take us to purgatory," demanded Merilee. "I want to see if it's real."

"Yeah," said the one called Carol, "It sounds pretty cool."

Before Dante could reply, Merilee pushed past him and made her way to his bedroom, the others following. She led them to the closet door. As she opened it, Carol turned to Dante and grinned, "Nice room you have here. I especially like what you've done with the chair and the way the various articles of clothing hang on it. It shouts bachelor, or," glancing at her friend beside her, "bachelorette."

"Oh, good one," said the other, "You're no Henrietta housekeeper either, as I recall."

They were both laughing as Merilee disappeared into the closet.

Chapter 33. Recruits

When Dante stepped through the portal into purgatory, he almost bumped into one of Merilee's friends who along with the others had frozen in disbelief at what they were seeing. "My god," shouted Merilee, "It is real!"

"What the hell," said the one called Carol as Tauren stepped up to her.

"This isn't hell, its purgatory," he said, a large smile lighting his face causing a couple of Merilee's friends to nearly swoon, "We can't tell you much about hell, but we think that's its portal," and he pointed to the circle in the sky with the flickering red and orange light.

Turning to Dante, he let go a roaring laugh, "This is quite interesting. You amaze me with your recruiting skills, champion. I must say, I didn't expect you to be able to do this so soon."

"Do this," groaned Dante, "I have no idea why they're here."

"But," grinned Tauren, "here they are. Your first five recruits."

Marilee and her friends were still immobilized, gazing wide eyed at the giant in front of them. Merilee was so right, he was gorgeous. And, so was the woman who came to stand beside him. Her body was perfect. Her muscles were obviously toned and well sculpted, but not overpowering. There was no mistaking this gal's fitness since she seemed dressed in revealing beach wear. Although the knee boots with their attached daggers were a nice touch. The Herculean dreamboat introduced her as Astrada. "Is she the one who does the training stuff. I'd go through hell to get a body like hers," said the one called Joan, speaking to no one in particular.

"Purgatory," corrected Tauren.

"What," asked Joan, a puzzled look on her face.

"As I said earlier, this is purgatory. We know nothing about hell, but you won't have to go through it for Astrada to get you fit. You will go through purgatory, however, and it won't be easy," said Tauren, unable to resist grinning at his own bit of humor.

"Come," said Astrada, "I'll take you to the armory to get you something appropriate to wear and look over the weapons for what will suit you."

"Weapons," giggled one of Merilee's friends as they followed Astrada through a nearby doorway.

Tauren walked over to Dante and asked him to join him for a little talk as they walked around the grounds of the Stade. He realized the ladies were an unplanned recruitment, but he expected they would hang around, at least until actual blood was drawn. It would be a beautiful dream for them when they returned to their earthly life. He had prepared some portals they could easily find and imprint the way in their minds. They wouldn't need encouragement. From the looks of them and their eagerness to follow Astrada, certainly suggested they would stick around. Tauren told Dante he had agents around the world recruiting for him, but Dante was responsible for his part of the world.

If he communicated the message clearly, there would be those who would rush to join. Many others would be curious. If they were interested enough to visit, most would commit. It was communicating the possibility that was important. Dante wasn't sure what it all meant. Was he to buy tv ads, or go out shaking hands? Tauren explained he was only advising him. As champion, Dante should be able to figure out what he needed to do.

He could see Merilee and her friends out on the field, laughing and shouting in sheer joy as Astrada put them through their paces. It was apparent Tauren was right, they would be regulars. He, on the other hand, had much to think about. Although he would have loved to join Astrada and Merilee and her friends in their workout, he had planned to spend some time with his friends Adam and Earl that afternoon, so he had to get back.

"Don't worry about your lady, Merilee and the others. They will pass through your closet portal, but they will leave straight away with only vague memories of it. When they choose to return here, they can do so through other portals, or if you wish, you can have them pass through yours. You are the champion, on earth as in battle, I defer to your judgement."

Earl had scored tickets to the hockey game. It was a minor league game, but the players on the teams were worth watching. Some were on their way up to the next league, the proverbial big time, some were on their way out and others were perennial stalwarts of their respective teams. The caliber was good and Dante and his buddies, Adam, and Earl, never missed a chance to go when they could get tickets. So, it would be a full evening, dinner and drinks in the arena lounge, the game, and then a visit to one of their favorite restaurants, slash, pubs before calling it a night.

Dante was hoping he could interest the two of them in helping him out in his recruiting. Knowing them, they would be happy to follow him, but the sum total of seven recruits would not do much to bolster the defense force. He would turn to them to help him recruit. If they joined the ranks and he expected they would. That is if he could convince them he wasn't delusional, they would help him.

Adam was the ad guy; hopefully he would have some idea how to drive recruitment. The problem was this had no relation to any form of traditional recruiting. Convincing someone such a place as purgatory existed would be a chore. Even for those who believed in a purgatory, to claim the living could go there, too, would be a hard concept to get across. That it needed warriors to defend it from other sentient creatures from other purgatories would, to most, border on being an airy fantasy. Even after all this time, putting purgatory into a twenty-first century perspective, having experienced the reality of it, still seemed, for Dante, when he tried to articulate it, absurd. His friends would probably think he had plummeted off the deep end, or whatever the current idiom was for being crazy.

Nonetheless, Dante was determined he would give them the full story and spent the rest of the day before meeting up with them, preparing himself for the skepticism and ridicule he would likely meet. Taking a deep breath as he stepped to the door, he thought to himself, "well, here goes nothing."

He would meet his friends momentarily in front of the arena. The bistros and concessions always opened a little over an hour before 'puck drop'. He decided to broach the subject over a post meal drink, just before making their way into the stands at game time. Whatever happened, it better be a damn exciting game, or it might get darned uncomfortable. How he would explain it still concerned him as he neared the crowd outside the arena complex when he heard a familiar voice call out, "Hey, Wichita, over here."

Over by the main doors, he saw Earl and Adam furiously waving. "Damn it," Dante muttered to himself as he waved back, "Why did I choose Wichita?"

Chapter 34. Mad Man

The food, as always, was excellent in the arena lounge. The conversation not quite up to the same standards with Adam and Earl. There were a lot of tasteless jokes about Wichita, some less than scintillating stories by Earl about the girls he had gone out with recently, most fictitious.

Adam was excited because Valeri Karparov had been sent down by his major league club for conditioning before returning after a serious injury in the previous year's playoffs. The talk at the table bounced from Wichita, to dream girls, to great young hockey players, and Dante was beginning to believe he wouldn't be able to get a word in, let alone explain about purgatory or encourage his friends to help promote recruitment.

Dante could barely say, "I wasn't really in Wichita, I was in purgatory," when the first buzzer rang, and Adam rushed out to the stands to watch the warmup.

"Can't wait to get a look at Karparov; see if the old speed is back," he called back as he went through the gateway to get to his seat.

The game was exciting, and Karparov was even better than Adam expected. He set up two goals and eventually scored the winner. On the way to the bar, that was all Adam and Earl could talk about. They relived the game right down to Karparov's minutest movements as he flew past the defense and faked the goalie, sending him to his stick side and flipping the puck over his outstretched arm and into the net. This was Dante's wedge, "Hey, you know how important good defense is. I'm looking for good defenders. You guys interested?"

"What are you talking about, man? You know I haven't learned to skate backwards, and Earl can't stop on skates," said Adam, "I suppose while you were away you learned to play at a professional level and are about to be drafted."

"No, really, I'm looking for people interested in learning to fight. You'll learn to use blades, but not on your feet."

Moments later inside the bar, Dante was explaining to Adam an Earl all about purgatory, the coming invasion, and the need for warriors. A couple of failed attempts to turn the discussion into a comedy routine quickly faded and before long, the two friends were listening in silence, their jaws dropping. Their friend was too serious, and they couldn't help but believe him.

Before they knew it, they were writing down locations of portals and Adam was using his media awareness to plan out an ad campaign to have interested potential recruits make their way to purgatory. "Social media is the way to go," Adam gave a knowing grin, "We put the info out there and those it resonates with will be through those portals as soon as they figure out, they could be real."

The whole concept was too wild for Earl. He began singing Highway to Hell, and he sang it loud. And he sang it repeatedly. To be honest, he didn't sing the entire song, just kept repeating the familiar chorus. It was annoying to Dante and Adam, but it became really annoying to a couple of guys sitting at the table next to them. These were men who didn't take kindly to annoyances.

Adam had offered his advice, and Dante could tell he was very interested in joining his friend in the mysterious domain. Earl was still doing the mind-numbing chorus of Highway to Hell. Dante was sure Earl with his raucous musical styling was signifying his plan to commit as well. The two at the next table were, themselves, on the highway to hell. One of them turned to Earl, "Hey bud," he snarled, "You want to give it a rest?"

If Earl had heard him, he may have stopped, or at least tried. Sometimes he could get quite deep into a rut. Instead of toning down, he got even louder. The one who had spoken stood up to face Earl, fists clenched, "I said to give it a rest, Buddy."

Earl, in a moment of stubborn resistance, faced the complainer and repeated the musical phrase one more time. "Asshole," shouted the complainer, and he took a swing. Earl danced back, just slightly out of reach, and Dante jumped to his feet. Patting Earl on the shoulder, Dante asked him to stop then faced the complainer saying, "OK, man, cool down. My friend is a bit overwrought; I'll calm him down."

"Damn right he'll calm down, but I'm gonna do it not you," said the guy beside the complainer who stood up, raised two huge fists, and stepped towards Earl and Dante. This was a big guy, and his friend who had made the original complaint stepped forward alongside him, his fists raised, too. Dante immediately realized they were not merely upset with Earl's annoying song, but were, in truth, spoiling for a fight. He would not let this happen. The big guy jabbed at Dante while the other took a second swing at Earl. Dante saw both punches coming, pushed Earl out of the way, twisted sideways inside the big guy's jab and ducked under the other's swing. In a flash, he was between the two and snapped out his elbows at a carefully determined angle to catch each of the attackers at a pressure point on the side of each head.

The two crumpled back into their seats, unconscious. It was done so swiftly and with a minimum of contact that even someone watching would think the two would be assailants had backed down. Of course, in a moment, their heads would loll to one side or other and they would either tumble to the floor or be on their feet looking for vengeance. "Let's get out of here," cried Dante to his two friends. Throwing a couple of twenties on the table, he quickly directed them toward the door.

Outside, they were across the parking lot and nearly to Adam's car when they heard a voice behind them. "Hey, guys, wait up. I gotta talk to you."

They ignored him as Adam fumbled in his pocket for the key. The delay was enough to let the person calling get to them. Dante braced himself for action, but the man raised his hand, "Hey, take it easy, I just want to talk to you," looking at Dante intensely he asked, "Where you in the service, one of the black ops groups? The way you took those two guys out, I've never seen anything like it."

Dante sized up the stranger. This guy was fit. "Man, I couldn't believe my eyes. I learned a lot of techniques in MARSOC, but nothing like that," the stranger added.

"You want to learn this stuff? It's all hand to hand, no guns, bombs, or rocket launcher, just your hands swords, daggers, maces, spears," said Dante.

"Sounds challenging, but why no guns?"

"Don't work where we fight," Dante smiled, "If you're interested?"

"Hey, sounds cool, and if I can learn that move you used, I'm in."

Dante asked Adam, who had now gotten the car open, for a piece of paper. He took a pen from his pocket and wrote something down on the paper and handed it to the guy. "Go there tomorrow," he said, "walk into the alley and keep walking till you reach the training grounds."

Waving the paper at Dante, the guy smiled, "You bet, buddy, I'll be there."

"We'll see you then," said Dante.

"What?" Said Earl who hadn't really followed much of the conversation over the evening.

Chapter 35. Defenders

The shock Adam and Earl felt at first stepping through a portal into purgatory was eased by both the presence of a super-confident Dante at their side, and the sight of Merilee and one of her friends busily engaged in a furious duel with wooden practice swords. "Hey," it's Merilee," said Earl, "what's she doing here? And he waved, shouting, "Hey Merilee."

She stopped what she was doing and saluted Earl and Adam with a raised sword. When Astrada made her way over, Earl's eyes went wide, "My god, you are beautiful, and I mean beautiful."

"Why, thank you," smiled Astrada and she took his arm, causing Earl to nearly melt, "I have something I'd like to show you. Come with me."

Moments later Earl was racing across the large practice field, Astrada loping casually beside him, her ever present sword brandished and waving. She ran with him a few times across the field, then went back to Dante. "Well," she said, "he's in somewhat better shape than you were when you first arrived," and turning to Adam indicated he join her and Earl.

As it had been in the early days with Dante, the intensity of Astrada's training methods had them staggering around in pain between sessions. This discomfort would continue until their conditioning reached the point where it meant moving on to self-defense.

Adam's ad campaign proved successful. Early on the new recruits trickled in, wide eyed and uncertain about what was going on. As they adjusted and grew to enjoy the intense, but productive training, Adam discovered something interesting about his advertisements on social media. Not only were there many more new arrivals as the social media ads were doing what Adam had hoped but Adam discovered he was receiving emails from across the country. Even more surprising emails were coming in from all around the world asking about where they might find a nearby portal. Apparently, there were lots of folk out there interested in the proposition of learning warrior skills and joining a well-trained defense group.

In response, Adam and Dante sat down to do some research and were able to find directions to portals worldwide. Adam then set up the information so everyone requesting a local portal could find one. The recruits, mainly men, but a surprising number of women, kept pouring in. Perhaps many came because they were misfits in the world, but felt at home among the living in purgatory, while many others were enthused by the variety in the training regimen. Whatever their reason, most stayed. Those that didn't stay had come with their guns and were disappointed they wouldn't fire in this place. The Guardian and the Champion and their closest associates were happy to see those ones gone because they knew they had only come because they were looking for somewhere to legally kill and would resist giving up their guns.

After a while, time being relative in purgatory, earth's purgatorial domain had a large and well-trained legion. It was in no way a match for the numbers and viciousness of Fluglaz's warriors, but in Tauren and Astrada's view, Astrada having firsthand knowledge of Fluglaz's warriors, earth's legion was ready to meet and match them on the battlefield. It was a good thing, too, because word had come from the neighboring domains that a large advance party of Fluglaz's warriors would soon arrive at their boundary.

Dante and Astrada gathered an expeditionary team composed of some of earth domain's very best warriors to meet the enemy before they were too close. A tribute to Astrada's training technique, Merilee and her friends Carol and Joan were, along with Earl, an integral part of the group. The skill they demonstrated with a variety of weapons was amazing, and their hand-to-hand combat was without peer. Ability wise, Astrada felt no concern for their fighting skills, attacking and defending. They would not be easy opponents for even the fiercest of Fluglaz's warriors.

With the element of surprise on their side, along with the sheer talent of each and every one of earth's warriors, raised the odds of victory, at least with the Grand Duke's advance party. Only Dante had any shadow of doubt. While he knew and admired the capabilities of all the expeditionary group. From personal experience he also knew they were, as yet, unbloodied. How would they react when they needed to take a life? He could only hope that he and Astrada, along with those few warriors who had military experience back on earth, could keep them calm and focused. Let them take the time to work through it after the enemy was eliminated.

It was also possible some having been killed would be back in purgatory among the ranks of the atoners. If they could then make their way back to the Stade Arcanium, they might help defend once the invasion was underway, Dante realized thinking too much about this was unproductive. Until engagement with the enemy, there would be no useful answers to these concerns.

Meanwhile, Astrada gave them a rundown on what they would fight. "Mostly, the warriors you will meet will be similar enough to yourselves, but physically broader and slightly taller than the average citizen of earth. They are muscular with large heads and prehensile fangs. Most of them will have had their fangs docked as flashing full-fledged fangs is considered crude and unseemly among the populace. Even flattened they can do serious damage so try to keep clear of their jaws. Other than that, their vital organs are in about the same place. If you're in close quarters, move fast and stab. Whatever you do, don't slash without a two-handed grip. Their skin is leathery."

The expeditionary corps were preparing to mount up and head towards the edge of the domain, there to await their instructions to proceed against the approaching invaders. The members were experiencing various degrees of anticipatory enthusiasm and trepidation. They were fully aware of their skill and certain in their readiness. It was the waiting for final instructions that made them anxious. So, when the word finally came, they didn't delay, but mounted their horses right away and were heading for the no-man's-land separating earth's domain from its neighbor.

They were ready for anything. The inhospitable terrain between the domains didn't deter them, and neither did the ever-expanding dimensions of the surrounding land. It just meant their journey would take a little longer. It also told them that like earth, the neighboring domain was still vital. It didn't deserve to be invaded by Fluglaz during his empire building, not that any domain, new or ancient, did. If Dante's expeditionary team could help preserve the independence of the neighbors' domains, it would make the coming fight even more necessary.

Chapter 36. Another Champion

Arriving at the threshold of the neighboring domain, a rag-tag group of armed men met Dante's expeditionary team. To Dante's eyes, they looked as human as he was. If there were any differences, they were invisible to him. A young, blonde-haired lad stepped forward. He held a sword in his hand; the blade dragging on the ground. It horrified Astrada to see this. Her trainees would never dare to hold their sword in such a graceless manner. "Are you invading us?" asked the young man, "I heard invaders were coming. The Guardian told me."

"We are not the invaders, you were warned of," responded Dante, "we are on our way to meet them and hopefully turn them back."

"The Guardian told me they were insidious. They won't stop until they conquer as much of purgatory as they can. He also said there was no way we could stop them," The blonde youth nearly broke into tears, "But we will try."

"Where are your warriors," asked Astrada.

"These are them," he pointed to the mix of living and atoners standing behind him.

There couldn't have been more than fifty, and those holding weapons were clearly untrained. Some didn't even know how to properly hold the weapons they carried. Dante's team consisted of at least three hundred highly trained warriors. Nearly ten thousand skilled defenders guarded the boundaries back in earth's domain. If this was the sum total of this domain's defense force, it was pathetic. Fluglaz's advance group would deal with them in short order and be on their way.

"Where is your Guardian," asked Dante.

"He's in the temple. He said we must be prepared for the inevitable and is hiding what he can of our nation's artifacts from the new rulers." the boy shook his head in disbelief as he spoke.

"Your champion, is he about," asked Dante, "I would like to speak to him."

"I am the one they call the champion," said the youth.

Dante looked toward Astrada and shook his head. This was the champion of the domain, a boy who looked to be barely sixteen and a group of armed, but otherwise unprepared volunteers. Among the group, he could clearly identify several atoners. It sounded as if the Guardian had been collecting artifacts and was now more interested in preserving them from the coming invaders than protecting the domain. The atoners could not leave the domain, and one look at the living defenders suggested pretty much the same for them. Their defense would be fragile and short-lived, their attack non-existent.

Dante dismounted and stepped up to the blonde-haired youth. "I am the champion of earth's realm," pointing at the warriors lined up behind him, he added, "And this is my expeditionary team. They are our most skilled warriors. We are not here to invade you; we just seek passage through your domain to repel the invaders before they can enter."

"You know where they are?" asked the young champion.

"I am told there is a small mountain just beyond your borders and they approach to the right of that."

"I know the place. I can guide you if you let my fighters ride along," said the youthful champion.

"We appreciate your offer and since it is your domain, your fighters are free to ride with us, although I don't believe any of them should go beyond the boundary. Oh yes, and for the sake of our warrior chieftain," Dante pointed to Astrada who nodded, "please don't drag the tips of your sword on the ground. Either sheath them or carry them across your body," and he drew his own sword to demonstrate.

The ride across the domain was uneventful. The structures they saw looked much like the ones in earth's purgatory, but with a slight twist. There was an alienness to them the earth humans could not quite explain. The people, too, primarily atoners, while looking in every obvious way the same as the people of earth, seemed to carry an aura of alienness. Despite this, the people of this domain would fit easily among the people of earth. The steeds the young champion and his follower's rode were more clearly alien. Their bodies were sleek. Long necks, crowned with a mane extended to a more feline looking head. They did not run on hooves, but thickly padded, three clawed paws.

As they rode, the two champions spoke. Dante learned from his youthful counterpart who referred to himself as Yvax, that his world and his people were far more peaceful than those of earth. There had not been a war or rebellion of any size for the equivalent of many hundreds of years. Crimes of passion were few and soldiering, neither necessary nor of interest to anyone. Few of Yvax's people, among the living or among the atoners, had even the slightest idea of warfare, weaponry, or any other form of combat. Even fights were rare. Despite this, it was no paradise and far from crime free, just as harmful to the populace, but generally less violent.

This explained the unpreparedness of the entire population of the domain, as well as Yvax and his rag-tag band of armed supporters. That they would take up arms in a feeble show of defense was a tribute to their loyalty and courage.

Reaching the further boundary of the domain, Yvax, in agreement with Dante, ordered his followers but for two of the most capable of the living to remain just inside the border, while he and his two fellows guided Dante's troop to the right side of the mountain where Fluglaz advance war party was approaching.

Arriving at the foot of the mountain, the members of Dante's expeditionary force sight out locations where they could set their defenses, prepare their attack, and wait for the arrival. Within a short time, the three hundred warriors were out if sight, hidden from the eyes of Fluglaz's advance troop's scouts. What was of further benefit to Dante's band, the advancing troop had grown complacent. They had never encountered a serious defense from any of the domains they had penetrated and held for the arrival of their legion. The scouts were sloppy. Not only could they not see the hidden warriors in their defensive positions, but they didn't bother to screen the location as a potential risk. Cocky in their scant evaluation, they returned to the larger contingent with word that there was a smooth passage to the next domain just ahead.

The commander of Fluglaz's advance troops was a hardened veteran of many encounters. Most of them in the fiercely competitive regions near the home domain. Even he had been lulled into unpreparedness by the nearly non-existent resistance he had encountered on this extended operation.

As they approached Dante's position, they were relaxed and confident expecting no significant opposition, at least none they couldn't easily handle. They were especially unprepared to meet opposition in the no-man's-land beyond the borders of the next domain.

The sight of dust rising up in clouds in the distance told Dante when the hostile forces were getting near. Word was quickly passed through the ranks to prepare.

Chapter 37. Faster, Smarter, More Skilled

As Fluglaz's 'storm troops' came into view under the soft and shadowless light of purgatory, they were a sight to behold. The staccato beat of drums preceded their coming into sight. The first thing Dante and his team saw were the many banners flown by outriders on either side of the main body. Light reflected off their highly polished body armor. Dante understood that even at this distance, such a display would, as intended, strike fear into the ranks of even the best prepared defenders.

When the enemy, themselves, were clearly in view, they were hideous. Even Astrada's thorough description didn't do justice to their fearsomeness. Their bodies were well muscled and broad enough that two humans could stand behind them side by side and not be seen. The bits of grey, leathery skin showing around their helmet and body armor looked to be impenetrable. Their heads were enormous, and Dante wondered how strong their neck and back muscles must be to keep that monstrous head erect.

As Astrada had explained earlier, they flattened their fangs. He could see the fangs of those nearest. They implanted their flattened fangs with bits of silver, gold and precious stones, the variety of which showed rank and social position. They were like tattoos on fearsome Russian gangsters. As the invaders came closer, Dante and his warriors could see they all had highly ornamented fangs.

As the fearsome troop approached, Astrada, moving swiftly and carefully, was reminding her warriors not to submit to fear at the sight of their opponents, "Remember, she kept saying, you are quicker, smarter, and more skilled than any of them. They have never learned the fine points of one-on-one fighting because they never needed to. This makes you, in every way, better."

As yet unbloodied, but feeling confident, Dante's expeditionary forces waited quietly as their adversaries came nearer. They would wait until Dante delivered his ultimatum to the invaders, requesting them to turn around and return whence they came. None believed they would do that and were prepared on the enemy's first attack to retaliate with crossbows, with the intention of both taking out as many riding animals and leading warriors as possible before turning to hand to hand combat.

Dante, from his location slightly forward of his fellows, did not show himself as he delivered the ultimatum. The words barely uttered, the air was filled with the sound of spears clattering against the rocks. The enemy began a charge, but before they could near Dante's position, they were met with a rain of crossbow bolts. The huge beasts they rode were collapsing to the ground while those behind stumbled over their writhing bodies. Many on the front line of the attack were either dead, wounded, or pinned under the twisting bodies of their riding beasts.

The ones behind dismounted and continued their charge. Crossbow darts fell a good number of them, then Dante's warriors rose from their hiding and with swords and daggers and some with axes and maces ran forward to meet the oncoming enemy. The battle was short and fierce. Astrada was right, Fluglaz's warriors were slow and lacking in skill. Still, they were ferocious fighters.

Earl was busy with a hostile warrior who had made a lucky hit on Earl's side and was pressing. Despite the wound, Earl was still faster and was easily besting his opponent when another came up behind him and raised his sword above his head for a killing stroke. Merilee was there at that moment and drove her sword deep through his ribs and into his heart, sending him stumbling backwards, away from Earl. He hit the ground at the same time as his sword touched down behind him. At that moment, Earl was able to lunge and strike a vital organ in his opponent, who roared in amazement as he stared down, disbelieving at the sword buried deep in his chest. His thought at that moment was, "This was not supposed to happen!" and then he was back in his home domain, another atoner.

Earth's warriors were, as Astrada predicted, were quicker and more agile than their adversaries. They also wielded their weapons with superior skill and soon had the remaining members of Fluglaz's advance team on the run. In the heat of blood lust, Dante's warriors ran after them, cutting down as many as they could. Dante joined his fellows, knowing they could allow none of the enemy to escape and carry the message of their defeat back to the main legion. No longer troubled by the need to stop these proud invaders, he jumped in front of one after another, fending off their slashing blades and sending them back to atone.

Looking around, Dante saw the sandy terrain was littered with bodies. It proved to be almost the entirety of Fluglaz's elite warriors. The battle done; the members of the expeditionary force made their way back to where they had set their ambush. Among them, the energy and excitement had drained away. Many were hurting with wounds both minor and, in a couple of cases, severe. Joining them, Dante surveyed the scene. He could see Astrada tending to the wounded. Others were gathered around their fallen friends. When the count was finally taken, ten of Dante's expeditionary force were dead as were the youthful champion's two companions, many more were wounded.

Yvax strolled over to Dante. He was holding his arm, broken as he ducked to avoid the mace of one of the few survivors from Fluglaz's troop. Merilee's friend Carol had finished him off before he could hurt the boy further. "Thank you," he said, "You have saved our domain from invasion."

"Don't thank us yet," responded Dante, "This was a small advance troop, the larger legion will inevitably follow."

"Yes, I know," said the young champion, grimacing as he moved his arm to get more comfortable, "but I know what I must do."

"And what is that?" asked Astrada, as she tested his arm to find the break.

"Train a defense force like yours that would give us a fighting chance," gasped Yvax as Astrada's fingers pressed on the site of the break.

"How do you plan to do that?"

"We will need help. Can we talk when we get back to my domain?"

Dante smiled and nodded agreement, but right now he had more important things to do at the moment. He walked around to speak to the wounded. Earl was smiling as Carol fussed over his injury, but Merilee was devastated, Joan was dead. She had died protecting one of the fallen from two of Fluglaz's warriors. She had successfully killed both but was pulled down onto his dagger by one of them as he died.

It was a quiet ride back to Yvax's domain. The battle with the advance troops while short was ferocious, and they were tired and sad. They had lost friends. This was purgatory. They might see these friends again, but it would never be the same. When they got back to earth's domain, they might be up to celebrating their victory then. They would also need to prepare for the larger invasion force. As they rode, Yvax made his request. Would Dante teach his people how to fight like his troops do. "Any of these warriors could train your people assuming you can find enough to create a legitimate defensive corps," said Dante, "If you wish, I can ask for volunteers. It's all I can do. It will be up to them to agree or not."

In the end, four of Dante's troop, Carol being one of them, stayed. They would train potential warriors for this domain and teach them how to forge their own weapons. The remaining set off on the return trip for home.

Chapter 38. The Beginning

It was a low-key group of warriors that returned to earth's purgatory. Their first encounter with Fluglaz's invaders was a success, but there was no celebration. Ten warriors who had been friends and companions were dead. Yes, they were somewhere out there in the distant parts of earth's purgatory. Although it was possible, they might see some of them again, as atoners, they would be changed. They would have only a smattering of memories regarding their death and the life they lived before.

There was no time for revelry. Some members of the expeditionary force would return to earth's plane while others would sort through the things, they had learned from their encounter with Fluglaz's warriors. They all knew that whether anyone had carried back the news of the defeat of the advanced troop or not, Fluglaz's commanders would know a unit that size did not just vanish into the ozone. The element of surprise would never again be as effective.

Besides the military concerns, were some other equally significant ones. Merilee and Carol were concerned about how they would present Joan's death to her family and explain why there was no corpse. Both Adam and Earl suggested they not tell them, but Dante understood the effect of the silence on the family, the questions and concerns they would have would be more agonizing for them than facing the knowledge someone had been with Joan when she died and that the cause was good.

He encouraged Marilee, Carol, and the other friends to carry the news to them. It would take days to construct the story of her death so that the family would have some satisfaction. This was an issue with several others of the deceased as well. It was simply one more burden on the backs of the warriors of earth's purgatorial domain.

The sheer joy of training, as hard as it was, was gone. It now became a serious business. Astrada made it clear Fluglaz's legions were relentless. It was unlikely the loss of an advanced team would deter them. For Fluglaz and his commanders, the lives of their warriors meant nothing. Those warriors were the fodder that would help them achieve their goal. That goal was to conquer purgatory. Any defeat, even of an advance party of two or three hundred warriors, would only galvanize them. Their brutal march to conquest would continue. Fluglaz's invading legion would eventually make its way to Yvax's domain and if not stopped there, eventually, on to earth's. The prospect, while hardening the will of earth's warriors to resist, was also a daunting one.

Whatever the case, earth's defenders would be prepared. Speed and exceptional skill with all forms of weaponry was essential to success and so the warriors would continue to train under the watchful eye of Astrada, honing the skills and abilities that would give them any advantage over the ruthless and ferocious forces aligned against them.

So it was, with the bulk of the warrior representatives of earth's population having no need to return home immediately, they stayed on to continue their intense training. Those who needed to return to earth came back to purgatory whenever they could also to continue training.

Earl, still suffering from the wound he had received in battle, returned to earth to apply and receive a disability leave from work. He then went back to purgatory, where his wound would heal faster. Dante, Adam, and Merilee also went back to earth to, at least for the time being, continue their work for their firm and to continue recruiting.

After some discussion, Adam went back to purgatory and with a small detachment, made his way to Yvax's domain. There he sought out information, learning that the home world of Yvax and his people had a version of the internet that was showing the rudimentary beginnings of social media.

On learning this, Adam worked with Yvax and his people to set up a recruitment package on their version of the internet. The Guardian of the Yvax domain, while nearly invisible, did help to establish some portals for potential recruits to find their way to the training field. There, Carol and her associates were making some progress refining the volunteers' warrior skills. It was not a simple task given the peaceful nature of that world's denizens, but their desire to protect the domain was an excellent motivation.

Dante and Merilee were back at the bistro where Dante first broached the subject of purgatory. He had another subject to discuss, and despite who he was and everything he had gone through, he still broke to in a nervous sweat. Up to that point the conversation flowed smoothly between them, but suddenly the words wouldn't come. Forcing a deep breath, he finally stuttered out the question that had been nagging him for days now. At first it came out in battle terms, "M-M-Merilee, w-w-would you ride with me as my lieutenant, my right hand, m-m-my c-c-companion... not only in battle, but always?"

Merilee had to laugh. This big, blubbering idiot was earth's champion. Then she softened and leaned over the table to give him a kiss. "Of course, I'll ride with you, or walk, or even sit around with you Dante," she paused, gave him another kiss and added in a diffident tone, with a huge grin and her tongue planted solidly in her cheek, "It would be and honor to be your companion my champion."

"Please don't," groaned Dante, "I'm just Dante and I'm the one who is honoured."

Merilee couldn't stop laughing but not at his request. That filled her with joy, but at the ingratiating sweetness of his bashfulness. Not long after, they were back in purgatory at a planning session with Tauren, Astrada. Adam and some other experienced tacticians. Fluglaz legion would soon arrive at the boundary of Yvax domain. They had to do everything they could to be ready.

Although fewer in numbers than earth's defensive forces, Yvax now had a well-trained force prepared to defend their border with skill and genuine resolve. A large contingent of earth's warriors would shortly be on their way to bolster Yvax forces.

In a large room, several domains away, the commander of Fluglaz's legion and his executive officers were meeting to plan their own strategy. "Why," asked one of them, "have we not received a report for the advance party yet. They should have taken the place and sending back a messenger by now."

"The advance troop comprises our most elite warriors," said the commander, "they have always been very efficient at taking the Guardian's capital in each domain which is their prime objective. Once they have secured it, they immediately sent messengers back to tell the legion to proceed," pausing briefly to express the point, he then added, "Since none has come back to report yet, we must consider that they have met some opposition."

"They don't have the numbers or the equipment for an extended siege," said another, "they should have sent word back for support by now."

"Well, then," said the commander, "we must assume that they are in no position to do that."

"That means...."

"Yes," said the commander, "it means they have met serious resistance and have been defeated."

"But, no one came to inform us."

"Because," said the commander, "they are most likely all dead."

"Then we must send a message back to the emperor to send us more warriors."

"And, while we do," added the commander, "We proceed, carefully, in the knowledge there is a worthy enemy out there. We will mobilize as soon as we can and proceed with the understanding there could be a well-prepared force of hostiles out there and be ready for a ferocious encounter at any moment."

Fluglaz's legions were each made up of several thousand warriors, many were out among the citizens of their conquered domain, demonstrating to the residents the brutality and mindless cruelty that was their hallmark. The word went out to assemble and be prepared to march. It would take time to get them all back and ready to move, but soon enough it would happen. Scouts from Yvax domain returned to him and his earthly allies with the news the legion threatening them would soon be on the move.

Dante stood, his arm around Merilee's waist, at the boundary of earth's purgatory, gazing out into the no-man's-land between theirs and Yvax domains. Tauren and Astrada stood nearby. "They are coming soon, and they are prepared for us. We must be ready."

Don't miss out!

Visit the website below and you can sign up to receive emails whenever Mick MacNeil publishes a new book. There's no charge and no obligation.

https://books2read.com/r/B-A-RHTQ-APNTB

BOOKS 2 READ

Connecting independent readers to independent writers.

Also by Mick MacNeil